CRAZYLEGS MERRILL

CRAZYLEGS MERRILL

By Bill J. Carol

Steck-Vaughn Company · Austin, Texas

Library of Congress Catalog Card Number 79-76609

Printed and Bound in the United States of America

1

A SPIRITED SCRIMMAGE was in progress, and the Pine Ridge quarterback had just thrown a sideline pass. But since he had been rushed quite effectively, he had thrown the ball much too far. Nevertheless, the football attracted a crowd of perspiring football players, who pounded directly toward Gene Merrill—a spectator watching from the sideline.

As the stampeding herd grew closer to Gene, he looked up to see just how much the football had been overthrown. Coming to a quick decision, he dropped his World History text to the ground and sprinted away from the playing field. Despite a noticeable limp, his long legs covered the ground swiftly. Racing under the football, he reached up and pulled it down.

Almost at that same moment he was struck from behind. The ground slanted up toward him. Even before he struck it, however, another driving body slammed into his left side. When he hit the ground, he was tumbling, both arms wrapped about the football. Another Pine Ridge player tried to avoid his rolling body by leaping to one side. But he was not fast enough, and Gene felt the boy's legs buckle as Gene struck him.

When Gene got to his feet, he shook his head groggily, tossed the football to an approaching Pine Ridge player, and started back to where he'd dropped his World History text.

"Thanks, Crazylegs," said the player as he caught the ball. The fellow had a wide grin on his dirty face. "Nice catch."

Gene acknowledged the player's remark with a nod, but said nothing as he continued on past him. He felt a little groggy from the tumble he had taken.

"All right, Merrill! What's the big idea?"

Turning, Gene saw the Pine Ridge coach storming across the grass toward him. Coach Linardi was an enormous man with broad, hefty, rock-like shoulders. Local legend insisted that when he'd played football in college, he hadn't needed shoulder pads. He was wearing a tan baseball cap, a white sweatshirt, and clean, sharply pressed khaki pants.

Gene stopped. The coach seemed quite upset. "You want to get killed," he demanded, "trying a crazy stunt like that?"

Gene shrugged. "No," he said. "I don't want to get killed. I just thought I'd catch the ball."

Gene had spoken quietly, reasonably—and his

answer seemed to rob Linardi of most of his steam. The man took a deep breath; then, shaking his head in exasperation, he walked on past Gene toward one of his players still on the ground.

When Gene reached the spot where he had dropped his book, he found it gone. He turned in surprise and looked up and down the sideline. Who would want to take a World History text?

"Looking for this?"

Gene turned to see Ronny Kline walking toward him with the history text in his hand.

"I saw you drop it," Ronny explained, handing it to Gene, "so I picked it up for safe-keeping."

"Well, thanks, Ronny," Gene said, taking the book from him. "What're you doing out here?"

"Watching the scrimmage like you. Only I was watching from down there." He turned and with a nod of his head indicated a small group of boys and girls sprawled on the grass close to the end zone. Ronny looked back at Gene. "Barbara Collins is down there with us. In fact, she was the first one who noticed you standing up here alone."

Barbara's name agreeably alerted Gene, but before he could respond, the coach's rough voice broke into their conversation.

"Hold it right there, Merrill!"

Gene turned. The coach seemed even more upset than before, but this time he seemed to be making a determined effort to keep himself under control.

"What's the matter, Coach?"

"My left end, Marble—the player you knocked down. He's out of it. Looks like a pretty serious knee injury."

"Oh, golly! I'm sorry, Coach."

The coach stopped in front of Gene. "Will you just tell me what in Sam Hill made you go after that football?"

Gene shrugged. "It was way out of bounds. And it was plenty high, so I figured I'd go get it for you."

"You mean you figured you could catch it, so you went after it."

"Yeah. Well, I'm sorry, Coach. I didn't mean to hurt anybody. But those guys didn't have to follow me right off the field, did they?"

"No, I suppose they didn't."

The coach's eyes became thoughtful slits as he looked Gene over carefully from head to toe. Gene glanced nervously at Ronny.

"The trouble is," went on the coach, "your being sorry won't mend Marble's knee. Now what I'd like to know is what got into you? You've never played football, have you, Merrill?"

"Well—not exactly."

"Now just what do you mean by *that?*"

Gene was unsettled by the coach's response.

What did the man want from him anyway? He had answered the fellow as honestly as he could. He had *not* played in any football games this past summer. Nothing like that. But since last March he *had* been working out with Skip Wittington.

Skip had injured his knee in a game at State just before the Christmas holidays. Then he'd caught pneumonia. Weak and hardly able to get around, he'd been sent home to Pine Ridge to recuperate. Not until the last week of January had he been able to hobble about, and it was not until March that he felt well enough to throw a football.

While walking by Skip's house one day, Gene had been hailed by the tall Negro, who showed Gene his football, slapped him on the back, and pulled him into his backyard to practice. It was not long before Gene found himself looking forward to his daily workouts with Skip.

"I've been working out with Skip Wittington," Gene said, "if that's what you mean."

"Since when?"

"Since last March."

"He's been passing to you and you've been catching for him. I'd heard he'd been hurt. How is he now?"

"He's fine."

"But that limp of yours, Merrill. Doesn't it affect your running?"

"I had polio when I was younger, Coach, but it

doesn't really bother my running any. One leg's just a little bit shorter than the other."

"Which leg is shorter?"

"The right one."

The man nodded. "You're a sophomore. Right?"

"That's right."

"And you've never played in a football game in your life."

"No, Coach. I haven't. With this limp, I've—"

"Well, limp or no limp, you made a creditable catch back there. Maybe *you* ought to be my end instead of that crazy Marble. Well, I guess it wasn't really your fault, Merrill. Sorry I blew my stack. See you."

He turned and started back across the field.

"Wait a minute, Coach," Gene said. "Did you mean what you just said about my playing end instead of Marble?"

Linardi turned back to Gene. "What's that?"

"I asked if you thought I could play end instead of Marble."

The coach frowned, thought a moment, then brightened visibly. "You tell me. Do you think you could?"

"I'm asking you, Coach."

"Why, sure, I think you could. You interested?"

"I might be," Gene said, trying not to show his mounting excitement.

"Okay, then. Be out here tomorrow at two-thirty," the coach said. "We can't give you any uniform, you understand. So just wear your old clothes and a sweatshirt." He suddenly grinned broadly at a joke that only he seemed to appreciate, then he turned abruptly and trotted back across the football field toward the team.

The team was gathered in a large, anxious huddle, waiting for him.

Gene shook his head in disbelief as he watched the big man go. It was all so crazy—and wonderful, too!

"Honest?" said Ronny. "You really going to show up tomorrow?"

"Are you kidding? I'll be right here, wearing a sweatshirt and an old pair of slacks—just like the man said."

"Hey, that's great. Well, come on then. You can watch the rest of the scrimmage with us—maybe get a few pointers."

"No, Ronny. I guess I'll go on home now."

"What about Barbara?"

"Heck. I'd be too nervous to even look at her," Gene said.

Ronny laughed. "Okay, Gene. See you."

For a moment Gene stood and watched as Ronny walked down the sideline toward the small clump of students sprawled on the grass. He had no difficulty at all in picking out the red sweater Barbara had worn to school that day and her long, shoulder-length hair—a bright spangle of gold in the afternoon sun.

The moment Ronny reached the group, he bent to say something to Barbara. At once Gene turned and started back toward the school. Halfway to the school he found himself trying to walk without revealing his limp.

But it was no use, of course. He limped, and there was nothing he could do about it.

When he entered his mother's kitchen not much later, he knew for certain that she had baked a cake. The smell of it hung so heavily in the warm kitchen air that he imagined he could actually taste it, frosting and all.

Looking around, he spotted it quickly, a double-tiered, beautifully decorated masterpiece sitting on top of the refrigerator. The oven door was hanging open, and from its interior still drifted the aroma of warm cake. Somewhere in town there was a wedding or an important dinner, for no really special occasion was complete without a Ma Merrill cake.

"Ma!" he called.

"In here!"

She was in the bedroom off the kitchen. He walked in and saw her folding a box for the cake. She looked up at him and smiled. She was a tall, somewhat homely woman with a nose perhaps too large for her face and cheekbones a trifle too prominent. Nevertheless, though Gene had never really thought about it, her face had always seemed extraordinarily beautiful to him. More than anything else, it was the warmth in her eyes and in her smile, a smile so quick, so sad—so ready to understand.

"Just in time," she said. "You can take this cake over to the Grange for me."

"What's the big deal there?"

She finished building the box and straightened. She was a bit taller than her son, who was already close to six feet. "A testimonial dinner for Jackson Schwartz." She shook her head. "I hope the old buzzard isn't too excited to appreciate the extra eggs I whipped into it."

"Okay," Gene said. "I can leave right now, soon as I put this book up in my room. Where's Dad?"

"He's probably back down at the station. Why don't you stop on your way back and walk home with him? He's liable to miss supper if you don't remind him."

Gene nodded and started up the stairs to his room.

After delivering the cake to the Grange building on Market Street, Gene cut down Canal Street, moved across a vacant lot, and came out alongside the railroad tracks. The station house was directly ahead of him on his side of the roadbed.

Entering the building, he followed the path his father's footsteps had made across the dusty floor to the stationmaster's office and stepped into the familiar room.

Mr. Merrill was sitting at his old rolltop desk in front of an open window. "Saw you coming, Gene. Supper's ready, huh?"

Gene nodded.

"Be right with you."

Gene sat down in a dusty wooden chair by the desk.

"The five-twenty freight should be along pretty soon," his father told him. "I'd like to wait for it. It doesn't stop, but sometimes the engineer waves. I know the fellow from 'way back. Johnson, his name is."

"Sure, Dad."

In the dim room all that was clear to Gene was his father's head and shoulders, dark against the open window. He had opened it, Gene assumed, so that he could lean out and wave as the freight went by. They sat for a long while in the fading light without saying a word until at last his father broke the silence.

"Here she comes," he said softly.

And then Gene heard it too—a low rumble,

more like a mutter. A moment or two later came the first faint bleat. At almost the same instant the huge ugly snout of the Diesel came into view from around the bend in the tracks—the outer ones, those that were still reasonably shiny. Another, louder blast followed the first, causing Gene to grit his teeth.

His father got up quickly from his chair and leaned out the window. As the train approached, he raised his right arm and began waving. Gene watched the Diesel engine as it swept up the tracks toward them and saw an answering wave from the cab.

Mr. Merrill turned back to Gene, a broad smile on his face. "Okay, Gene, let's go. I'm starving."

By the time they stepped out into the daylight, the sun was low among the trees, and Gene was reminded suddenly by the ache in the pit of his stomach that he too was hungry. He glanced at his father. The man was dressed smartly and neatly as usual. He was wearing a white shirt and a black bow tie under the navy blue sweater that Gene had bought him for Christmas the year before. His dark pants were well pressed, and his black shoes were still polished brightly despite the long walk down to the station. He was an old man, but he stood erect and tall, taller than Gene's mother; and his face had a craggy look about it—like that of a cliff chiseled by the weathering of centuries.

He gave a quick look around, as if he were making sure that everything was in order before leaving.

As they walked along, Gene glanced over at his father. "Dad, why do you still come down here? It doesn't do any good, you know."

"You know that for a fact, do you?" his father replied, smiling ironically at his son. "Oh, I suppose I could just sit in my room. And some mornings I could spend on the benches in front of the courthouse, talking to the other retired gentlemen—The Old Timers' Club. Instead, I come here. Is that so bad? Here there are memories, Gene, fine, powerful memories—and perhaps a chance to hear again the thunder of steel wheels on steel rails. What's wrong with that?"

"Nothing, Dad," Gene said. "Nothing at all, I guess."

They had reached Washington Street by that time. As they started down the street, they passed Skip Wittington's house on the corner. Bill, Skip's brother, stepped out onto the porch.

"Hey, Gene! We just got a letter from Skip! He says to tell you he's made the team—first string. Says he's throwing as good as ever!"

Gene stopped. "That's great, Bill. Tell him to drop me a line."

Bill's mother hurried out onto the porch and

stood beside Bill. "Now you know Skip, Gene," she said. "It's hard enough to get him to write us. But I'll tell him."

"He'd rather phone—collect!" Bill said with a grin.

"Afternoon, Mr. Merrill," Skip's mother said. "How are you today?"

"Fine, Mrs. Wittington. How's Fred?"

She smiled. "He's still working on that idea you and he discussed."

Mr. Merrill frowned uneasily. "He's a dreamer. Tell him I said to forget it."

Her face fell. It was obvious she had hoped for a different response from Gene's father. "You tell him, Mr. Merrill. You could tell him better than I could. He's all excited."

Gene's father just waved his hand and continued on. Gene was really pleased at the news about Skip.

"Boy, that's great, real great," he said to his father. "Skip will be the first Negro to quarterback a State varsity. Pretty good, huh?"

"Is he *that* good, Gene?"

"Sure, he is. And boy, can he throw a football."

"Well, I suppose you should know."

"And that reminds me. The coach thinks it wouldn't be such a crazy idea for me to try out for end on the high school team."

"You? Play football? But what about your leg?"

"He doesn't mind at all about the leg, Dad."

"Well, I mind. And so will your mother. Forget about it, Gene. That right leg of yours is weak—and will be for the rest of your life. It would be plain foolhardy for you to go out there on that field and let yourself get torn up. You saw what happened to Skip last year—and he never got the polio in his leg."

"He's all right now, Dad. Good as new."

"No, Gene, and that's final. I'm sure your mother will agree."

"I'm sorry, Dad," Gene heard himself say, "but I think I'm going to show up tomorrow and try out for the team."

The old man stopped and turned to face Gene squarely. Gene returned the gaze without wavering. Abruptly the man looked away from Gene's steady eyes and started up again. And though Gene could not be sure, he thought he detected a gleam of sudden pride in his father's eyes.

"You know, Gene," his father said, "I was a pretty fine fullback in my day." He squared his shoulders and smiled down at his son. "Yessir—a pretty fine back. Just don't tell your mother, that's all. Let me handle that."

Gene was surprised at his father's reaction. He had been certain his mother would understand. It was his father he had been afraid of—and yet, here was his father taking it almost without a ripple and warning Gene about his mother.

Suddenly his father stopped and cocked his head. "Did you hear anything, Gene?"

"No, Dad. I didn't hear a thing."

The old man nodded and started up again. "That's right. There's nothing due through here until tomorrow at ten."

It was then that Gene realized how much he would give if—for his father's sake alone—he could make the trains stop at Pine Ridge again. Or, better yet, if he could get his father really interested in Mr. Wittington's scheme to open a bakery in Pine Ridge. But either seemed about as likely as his dream of some day being able to walk without a limp.

Better to stick to the dreams that were possible, he thought—like playing on the Pine Ridge football team.

2

GENE SHOWED UP promptly at two-thirty the next day, dressed just as the coach had suggested—in a sweatshirt, old slacks, and sneakers. Coach Linardi, however, seemed to have forgotten all about him, and Gene could not find him anywhere. He was not in his office, and Gene could find him nowhere on the field.

At last, feeling hopelessly out of place, he took a stand just outside the gym door as the football team stormed from the gym and charged across the playground toward the football field. Some players were hefting huge bags of equipment; others had one or two footballs tucked under each arm. All of the players were in full uniform, their shoulder pads giving them a sudden, enormous breadth of shoulders, their thigh pads filling out otherwise skimpy legs.

In some cases Gene found it momentarily difficult to recognize fellow classmates. Those few who recognized Gene seemed downright unfriendly.

The reason for this was obvious to Gene. They'd all seen him limping along the corridors of the Pine Ridge School. Many, when Gene was younger, had found amusement in taunting him, calling him "Gimpy" among other things. The name-calling and the taunts stopped, of course, as soon as Gene began to put on height and breadth. But Gene remembered the faces—each and every face, in fact—and they remembered him.

Now they were wondering what Gene Merrill was doing out on a football field.

When all the players had left the gym, Gene turned and started back inside, discouraged and more than a little dismayed—an uncomfortable feeling building within him that he was being kidded. He twisted inside at the thought. But as he started across the gym, he saw Coach Linardi entering from the other side.

"There you are!" the man said, his resonant voice filling the gym. "You ready to do some running? I want you to work out with Jim Martin, our second string quarterback."

Gene stopped in his tracks, relief flooding over him. "Sure," he said. "I'm ready."

"Great. Jim needs the practice and I want to see just how good your moves are. Maybe that was just a lucky catch yesterday."

"Suits me fine," Gene replied as he started across the field beside the coach.

Jim Martin turned out to be a surprisingly slight young man with dark hair and a thin, sallow face who didn't look any too healthy.

"Jim," Coach Linardi said, "I want you to meet Gene Merrill. He's the fellow I told you about. Give him a good workout, will you?"

"Sure, Coach. Be glad to."

Jim turned to Gene with a smile and stuck out his hand. The smile flickered in Jim's pale face like summer lightning, and he seemed genuinely pleased to meet Gene. His greeting was a hearty one, unlike those of the other players working out at the far end of the field—all of whom had given Gene the distinct impression that for Gene even to consider working out with them was a huge and not very funny joke.

Even the coach had seemed to be taking Gene's appearance lightly, though Gene's impression of this was admittedly only a fleeting one.

"I've seen you around, Gene, haven't I?" Jim asked.

"Yes, I suppose you have. I've seen you around, too," replied Gene. "You're usually in a big hurry with an armload of books. You're a junior, aren't you?"

"That's right. Only one more year to go. If I can last, that is."

"You'll last," said the coach. "Don't worry." He turned to Gene. "Okay, Gene, you've met them all now. So why don't you two get over to that field beyond the goalposts and get busy?"

Jim patted the football under his arm. "Come on, Gene. You heard the boss."

As the two started across the grass, Gene looked at Jim. "Is Linardi a good coach?"

"Sure. And a real slave driver, too," said Jim, "but that doesn't mean we don't have fun. It just means we work hard and get a lot accomplished. We've won all our scrimmages so far this fall, and except for the loss of Marble, we're in real great shape. I think we might even take it all this season."

"I'm sorry about Marble."

Jim's thin face cracked into a grin. "You mean you don't know what really happened there?"

"What do you mean?" Gene asked. "Sure I know what happened. I was there, don't forget."

Jim studied Gene's face for a moment, then said, "And you think it was all your fault."

"Of course. If I hadn't gone after that football, I never would have knocked Marble down."

"Well, yes, that's true enough—as far as it goes. But the ball was thrown way out of bounds. Marble never had a prayer of getting it—and everybody knew it. But when they saw you limping after it, they all decided to have some fun. It was Marble's idea, in fact. He called to the rest to give you a nice ride if you caught the ball. They did, too. They took you out with a vengeance—only it backfired on Marble. And now *he's* out."

This really surprised Gene. "You mean they were just having a little fun?"

Jim nodded. "Sure. They didn't like the idea of you trying to catch that pass. At first Linardi thought it was all your fault. But he found out soon enough what happened."

"I see."

"He was really mad at Marble. And the others, too, for pulling a fool stunt like that. He went over to see if you were hurt, but I'll bet he was as fierce as a tiger and didn't even let on he was concerned about you."

"You're right. He didn't. He started blasting away at me—asked me what in Sam Hill I thought I was doing."

Jim nodded. "Sounds like him. Anyway, when he came back he told Marble and the others it would serve them right if he actually *did* put you in a game while they watched from the bench."

Gene stopped abruptly and looked at Jim. The quarterback's words told him unmistakably that all his fears, building since two-thirty, were justified. This whole operation—Jim Martin working out with him and his being led to believe that he could make the team—was simply a lesson for Marble. And that was all it was. Coach Linardi had no intention whatever of considering Gene as a full-fledged member of the team, let alone actually putting him in a game.

Jim realized at once what Gene was thinking. He ran his fingers through his hair and looked with dismay at Gene. "Oh, golly, Gene. I didn't mean it to sound like that."

"I know you didn't. But don't be sorry. You've saved me a lot of grief. I'm just out here to teach Marble a lesson, period."

"Well, look at it this way, Gene. You haven't even played *once* in a regulation football game, have you? Not even sandlot football. Isn't it kind of crazy to think you could just come out this late and make the team—I mean, just like that?"

Gene could find no words to refute Jim. The boy was speaking the indisputable truth of the matter. Without another word he turned and started off the field toward the high school building. He was furious with himself. And he was ashamed that he had been such a fool to think he could play varsity football and to let himself be used this way by Coach Linardi.

"Hey, Gene!" Jim called. "Come back here, will you?"

But Gene did not stop or look back.

He went upstairs to the high school library and got a good start on that day's English assignment. Finding an empty table close to the window, he did his homework there and kept an eye on the football field while he wrote. When at last he saw the players streaming off the field toward the gym, he gathered up his work and left the library.

The answer to Gene's sharp knock came at once. "Come in!"

Gene pushed open the door to the coach's office and stepped inside. The coach was standing in front of a wall locker in the corner.

"Well, there you are," he said, glancing at Gene. "I thought you'd gone home."

Gene closed the door. "No, I didn't go home. I wanted to talk to you."

Linardi reached into his locker for his tie, then closed the locker door. As he looped the tie over his neck, he kept his eyes on the mirror attached to the side of the locker. "So talk."

"That was a dirty trick," Gene said. "A real dirty trick—letting me think you were really serious about wanting me to try out for the team."

Linardi finished adjusting his tie. Then he looked at Gene. "You think so, huh?"

"Yes, I do."

"And that's what you came in here to tell me?"

Gene was getting no satisfaction at all. He took a deep, frustrated breath. "Yes, that's why I came in here."

"Good," Linardi replied coldly, as his eyes met Gene's. "Now you've told me. Is that all?"

Gene nodded haplessly, his anger draining from him under the unrelenting force of Linardi's eyes. At the moment the man seemed capable of probing Gene's innermost thoughts. Abruptly his eyes appeared to soften.

"Tell you what, Gene," the coach said. "I'll admit it. Sure, I made a mistake in not leveling with you. And I'm perfectly willing to admit it. I *was* somewhat amused at your thinking one lucky catch like that could actually put you in the running for Marble's position, and I just didn't think you'd be such a touchy customer. I figured you'd shag a few passes, run around a while, get shook up in intra-squad play, and finally stop showing up—with no harm done. I guess I was wrong, huh?"

"I guess you were," Gene replied.

"Well, then, why not stick it out anyway? Show me up. Demonstrate what a poor judge of football ability I am. Surprise me. Show me that despite that limp of yours, and your almost total lack of experience, you *can* make the grade."

"No thanks, Coach."

"Now hold it, Merrill. Don't say no. Don't ever say no as quickly as that. Learn to say you'll maybe think it over. No sense in going around burning all your bridges."

Gene shrugged. "Okay, I'll think it over. But it won't do any good, Mr. Linardi. I realize now how silly I was to think I could make it with your team. It was just a crazy dream."

As Gene turned to leave, Linardi spoke again, gently this time, "Sure it was a dream, Merrill. But isn't that what always comes first—a dream?"

Gene pulled open the door and glanced back at the man. He was no longer angry at him. "But you've got to admit it—some dreams are real crazy."

He left the office, pulling the door shut behind him.

The TV was on, the announcer making his pitch to an empty room. As Gene moved through the living room, he turned it off and continued on into the kitchen. His mother was wiping off the counter beside the sink, and Gene could smell a pie in the oven. She looked up as he entered, then turned back to the sink counter.

"Home later than usual, aren't you?" she asked.

He moved on past her to the refrigerator, opened it, and pulled out a nearly full quart of milk. "That's right. I'm home later than usual."

She was using a small yellow sponge to wipe off the counter. She turned on the hot water, held the sponge under the faucet, squeezed it out, then placed it down on the drain board. "Don't drink from the bottle," she said as she reached across the sink for a freshly washed glass and handed it to him.

He closed the refrigerator door and took the glass from her.

"Your father said you were going to try out for the football team today," she said.

He poured the milk into the glass. "That's right. I was. But I changed my mind." He swallowed the milk in three enormous gulps, then looked at his mother. He couldn't be sure, but he thought he caught a momentary flicker of disappointment in her eyes.

"Well, I'm glad," she said, obviously relieved. "You're showing good sense, Gene. You don't want to do anything that might endanger your leg."

"That's right, Ma. I don't want to do anything to endanger my leg." He filled the glass a second time and emptied it just as swiftly. Then he re-opened the refrigerator, placed the bottle back on the top shelf, and closed the door.

"I'm going upstairs," he said. "I've got some homework to finish."

"There's a letter for you. I put it on your bed," she said. "It's from Skip, I think. He didn't put a return address on it, but the postmark is Hamilton. That's where the State University is, isn't it?"

"Sure! That's where it is," Gene replied, brightening at once. "Hey, that's great! I'll bet it *is* from Skip."

He took the stairs two at a time up to his small room—the only one on the second floor—and found the letter lying face up on his bed. He flung himself full-length across the bed and tore open the envelope.

Dear Gene,

Hey man, how's it going? I'm doing just great. I really am. And guess what? I'm on the squad and playing regular. That's right—first string quarterback! Not bad for a black boy from Pine Ridge, huh?

And I owe it all to you. Oh, man, we really worked out, didn't we? Day after day. But my arm is real strong now and so is my knee. I feel like I could throw a football right through a brick wall.

One thing though, I really miss having you to throw to—old glue-fingers. That's what I should have called you. I thought it was my throwing arm that made us look so good. You really know how to scoot, and then when you get to the ball you hang on to it. That's something these guys here aren't so good at.

Anyway, thanks a lot, Gene. You really helped me. Soon as I get the tickets for the game with Alfred Tech, I'll send them along to you and your folks. This will be the biggest game of the season for us. It might even be nationally televised. And this year we're going to win it, no matter what the sports writers say.

I figure your folks and mine could probably drive down to Hamilton together in that big car of yours. Be a lot safer than my old man's Ford. But we can talk it over when I come home Halloween weekend. See you then.

Your friend,
Skip

Gene rolled over onto his back and read the letter over a second time. Then he folded it carefully and put it back into the envelope. He'd answer it that night, he told himself, just as soon as he got something settled. He got up, looked out of his small window at the quiet street below for a minute or so, then left his room and went back downstairs.

The kitchen was filled now with the smell of the hot apple pie his mother had just taken from the oven. She was rolling out another pie crust on the kitchen table.

"Was it from Skip?" she asked, glancing up at Gene. There was a smudge of flour on her nose.

"Yes, it was. He'll be home Halloween weekend."

"That'll be nice."

"He says he's going to get tickets for us to the big game with Alfred Tech. Would it be all right, Ma, if we went to the game with his folks? Would you mind, Ma?"

His mother frowned and pursed her lips thoughtfully, but continued to roll out the dough. "It's a little early yet to make that kind of a decision, Gene. Besides, Skip may not be able to get the tickets. And of course your father may not want to go all the way to Hamilton. The weather might be bad, and you know how your father hates to drive in bad weather."

She glanced at the electric wall clock over the refrigerator. "Speaking of your father, would you please see if you can locate him? It's getting close to supper time. I think he's at the railroad station again."

Gene wanted to protest that his father could easily find his own way home—but he didn't want any more battles that day.

"Okay, Ma," he said. He turned and left the kitchen.

As Gene left the house, he felt strangely let down. Skip's letter had really excited him. It made him feel great to think that Skip had taken the time to write and thank him and tell him what a fine receiver he had been this past summer.

Furthermore, he was now going to send Gene and his family tickets to the biggest game of the season—and perhaps even of the Central Conference.

And that was what was wrong, of course. Those tickets and Skip's suggestion that his parents and Gene's go to Hamilton together to see the game. Gene—and his mother too, he felt certain—was immediately uneasy at the prospect of being seen driving off to Hamilton with the Wittingtons.

Gene stopped walking suddenly as the full realization of what this meant struck him. It sickened him; he felt both his fists clench in anguish. Did he *really* feel that way about being seen in public with the Wittingtons? Yes, he did! But how could he allow himself to feel this way? He was more than ashamed; he felt he had betrayed Skip. Worse, he had slapped Skip's hand away at the very moment the older boy was extending it to him.

And why? Because he was afraid! That was the reason, the only reason. He was afraid of what people would think—just as he had been this afternoon when he had turned away from Jim Martin and walked off the field. Why hadn't he accepted Coach Linardi's offer to stick it out and show them what he could do? Why hadn't he stood his ground the way Skip had always had to do ever since he first entered school in Pine Ridge? It all boiled down to that in the end, really—it was a matter of courage.

Gene started up again and turned down Washington Street. As he passed Skip's small house a little later, he saw Skip's younger brother working over his bicycle in the narrow driveway.

He turned in and walked up to Bill. "What's the trouble?"

Bill turned to him and said, "It's the chain. It came off."

Noting that the chain was not broken, Gene lifted the bicycle and turned it over so that it was resting on its handlebars and seat. Then he asked Bill if he had a wrench. Bill turned about and raced into the garage. When he returned with the wrench, Gene loosened the nuts on both sides of the axle. Slipping the wheel forward, he and Bill fitted the chain carefully over the teeth of the sprocket. After that he tightened the nuts on the axle and turned the bicycle right side up again.

"Thanks, Gene."

"Got a letter from Skip," Gene said, handing the wrench back to Bill. "Says he's going to send us tickets to the big game. We'll all be going to Hamilton together. Neat, huh?"

"Hey, that's great."

"And another thing. Don't tell him yet when you write him, but I might end up playing on the Pine Ridge team myself this season."

"Honest?"

Gene smiled. "Sure. But wait until it's official."

As Gene returned to the sidewalk and continued on down Washington Street, he felt his shoulders lifting and squaring. He wasn't going to be afraid any more—of his limp, of the other players on the team, or of counting Skip Wittington his friend.

3

"WELL! LOOKEE HERE!" cried Jeff Townsend. "Look who's back!"

The Pine Ridge quarterback had been passing a football around with a group of players. The moment he caught sight of Gene approaching, he had swung around to face him.

"We all thought you'd gone home to Mama," Townsend continued, placing his hands on his hips and looking Gene up and down. "You think you're ready now to play with the big boys?"

Townsend was a very handsome, extremely popular member of the team and of the Pine Ridge student body. His hair was light and tended to curl; his cheeks were almost rosy. When he smiled, he dimpled on one side, and this dimple—along with his light blue eyes—gave him an almost cherubic appearance.

Despite the fair hair, the blue eyes, and the dimple, however, Gene disliked Townsend intensely. He always had, ever since the sixth grade when Jeff Townsend had led a pack of older students after him. It had been a wet, muddy spring afternoon, and the chase had ended only when Gene slipped and fell into a mud puddle. The pack of boys had surrounded the puddle and, grinning happily down at Gene, had started chanting, "Gimpy-leg! Gimpy-leg! Hey-hey Gimpy-leg!"

Jeff Townsend's voice had outshouted all the rest until finally Gene had ended it by hurling himself, muddy clothes and all, at Townsend. He had not won the rough-and-tumble that followed and had in fact been blamed for the whole business before it was over. But from that time, there had existed no possibility of friendship between Gene and Jeff Townsend, only a wary, not quite comfortable, truce.

Now, apparently, the truce was over.

"Yes, I'm ready to play with the big boys," answered Gene, "but where are they?"

"Hey! He got you that time!" called someone from behind Townsend.

Townsend flung an angry look back over his shoulder, then glared at Gene. "You quit yesterday. So why don't you stay quit?"

"If you're the official greeter," Gene said, as lightly as he could, "then I'd say you were doing a very poor job."

"Who says you're welcome?" said a big fullback that Gene only vaguely recognized. As the fellow spoke, he took his place squarely beside Townsend. "We don't want any gimpy-leg players on our team. We don't need sympathy to win our games."

Gene's knees went suddenly weak, while at the same time a fire sprang up within his breast. Hardly aware that he was moving, he strode up to the fullback.

"You have got a big mouth," Gene said quietly. "And that must come from putting your foot in it so often."

"Back off, back off," the fullback muttered, taking a hesitant step backward.

"What is your name, Big Mouth? If we're going to play on the same team, I should at least know your name—unless you want me to keep calling you Big Mouth."

The fullback had a round, beefy face with small eyes set close together over a fleshy nose. His tongue flicked out nervously to moisten suddenly dry lips. "Get off my back," he said.

"What's your name?" Gene persisted gently, as if he were talking to a nervous child. "Mouth?"

"Aw, go ahead and tell him, Mouth!" someone shouted happily from the back.

Again moistening his lips, the fullback said, "My name is Ketchel. What's yours? Gimpy?"

Gene put his head down and drove forward as hard as he could into Ketchel's mid-section. The fullback was wearing shoulder pads, but the area around his solar plexus was not protected. Gene heard the sudden gasp and the quick expulsion of breath as his head burrowed into Ketchel's stomach. He kept driving and felt Ketchel stumble backward, then lose his footing.

Gene flung both arms then around Ketchel's body and drove still harder as the fullback crumpled heavily with Gene on top. The moment they hit the ground, Ketchel began swinging at Gene; but Gene stayed on top and had little difficulty in parrying his furious swipes. At the same time he managed to get in quite a few good pokes himself before a crowd of arms pulled him back and up onto his feet.

To Gene's surprise, the whole football team seemed to have gathered around in the short time that he and Ketchel had been mixing it up. Gene freed himself from the constricting arms just in time to see a red-faced Coach Linardi, flanked by his two assistant coaches, hurrying across the field toward them.

"Hey! What's going on here?" Linardi demanded, as he hurried up. Then he saw Ketchel slowly picking himself up off the ground. "Okay, let's have it, Ketchel. Who just ran over you?"

Ketchel looked murderously over at Gene. The coach followed his gaze. When he saw Gene, he nodded. He was not surprised to see him on the field, since Gene had spoken to him earlier in the day.

Linardi looked back at Ketchel. "You mean Gene Merrill ran over you?"

There was a roar of laughter at that, but the coach's upraised hand brought it to a quick halt. "All right. All right, you fellows. Let's have it—now!"

It was Jim Martin who stepped out of the crowd of players and gave Linardi the story. He told it exactly as it happened, quoting word for word. When he finished, he summed it up by saying, "Looks like Gene ought to try out for fullback as well as split end."

Linardi swung around to face Townsend. Gene could see that the coach was upset at what he had learned of Townsend's behavior. "Is that the way it was, Townsend?"

Townsend shrugged. "Merrill's touchy, that's all. He can't take a little ribbing."

Linardi nodded and turned back to Ketchel. "How about you, Ketchel? You think Gene's unduly touchy? You think he should have laughed uproariously when you called him Gimpy?"

Ketchel looked away from Linardi. "No," he said. "I guess not."

Linardi surveyed the lot of them, his angry gaze taking them all in. "Now, look here, you guys. The only way we can blow it this season is to start fighting among ourselves. Gene Merrill is here because I asked him to give himself another chance to make the team. If he can help us by catching footballs, I want to know. And I want him to be given the chance to show me—one way or the other. Is that clear?"

Every head nodded.

"Okay, then! Back off! Bury any private axes you're still carrying around and concentrate on one thing only, playing football!"

Immediately Linardi broke up the players into linemen and backfield men and sent them off with their coaches. Then he turned to Gene.

"Well, you're off to a flying start with this team. That is for sure. Want to throw in the towel?"

Gene shook his head decisively.

"Okay, then. Come with me and we'll get you fitted. Later this afternoon we're going to run through a few plays—with you and Cartwright, another player who's on the freshman team now and wants to try out for the split end spot. Maybe if you see how well Townsend can throw, you'll learn to respect the guy if not to like him. Let's go."

Gene nodded. Though he was willing to go along with Linardi concerning Townsend's ability, he doubted he would ever really respect him.

On the snap Gene launched himself from his three-cornered stance and started downfield as fast as he could go. He was running a fly pattern; and as the huddle broke, Townsend had reminded Gene that the ball would be out there and that Gene had better be on hand when it came down.

As Gene fled down the sideline, he found it maddeningly difficult to move freely—to really stretch his limbs and fly. He just couldn't seem to get loose under this constricting, inhibiting load of plastic shoulder pads and cotton padding he was wearing. He felt like a turtle trying to run while still in his shell. And he had the uneasy conviction that—like the turtle—he was making very little headway.

He looked back. Above the enormous hump that was now his left shoulder, he saw the ball rising sharply into the air. Just as in Townsend's other four passes to him, this one had been thrown exceedingly well and was almost as perfect a spiral as Skip threw. The ball rapidly grew larger. Recalling Townsend's warning, Gene began to dig even harder. But the football had really been thrown, and it looked to Gene as if the ball just might come down without him under it.

He couldn't let that happen. He couldn't. So far he'd done fine, and he intended to prove that he could stay ahead of Townsend's arm—no matter how good it was. Grimly he dug harder and stretched his legs to their absolute limit in an effort to devour more precious inches with each stride.

As he did so, he noticed the way he kept rocking slightly to the right. That gimpy leg of his. Was it really strong enough to take this sort of punishment? And then he was under the football, reaching up for it. The ball came down with surprising gentleness upon the tips of his outstretched fingers; but when he tried to pull it in, he lost what little control of it he had. Nevertheless, he kept driving and reached out again for the football. This time he managed to grab hold of it and smother it against his chest. Then, with both arms wrapped firmly around the ball, he pitched forward heavily to the ground. The ball still in his possession, he picked himself up and started back upfield.

Though a few of the players had insisted on resenting him, after each catch Gene had noticed that there appeared to be more and more players who seemed impressed in spite of themselves. Now, as he neared the waiting players, he was certain of it. From the sideline Coach Linardi bellowed, "That's the way to go get them, Merrill! Nice catch!"

"Sure," said Townsend, as the huddle closed around. "Nice catch—but Marble would have been waiting for it. What took you so long, Merrill?"

"I told you before. I'm not used to running with all this equipment on," Gene replied. "I'll get faster."

"Sure you will," said Ketchel, winking across

the huddle at Townsend. "But how long do we have to wait?"

Gene did not reply. He simply looked down at his shoes and leaned over as the others did to hear Townsend call the next play.

Cartwright had been on the field working out with the team when Gene arrived back in full uniform. Gene had watched Cartwright with interest—and some envy. But so far, Gene felt sure, he had done pretty well in comparison with Cartwright. For one thing, the pass patterns did not present much of a problem to him, since Skip had made it a practice never to throw a pass unless Gene was executing a pattern of some kind. Gene's only problem was—and would undoubtedly continue to be—Townsend's hostility. Unless he and Townsend could . . .

"Any time you're ready, Merrill!" Townsend barked, his voice cutting into Gene's thoughts.

"Sorry," Gene replied. "Let's have it again."

"Button hook. First down special. On five."

The huddle broke. "First down special" meant that Gene was to race out about thirteen yards beyond the line of scrimmage, then execute a sharp about face and come back for the ball, which he should receive just beyond the ten yards needed for the first down.

On the snap, Gene took off. When he reached

what he considered to be thirteen yards, he spun about—and saw the ball inches from his chest. He had no time to defend himself, let alone reach up for the ball.

The football struck him squarely in the chest and bounced high into the air. Gene made a belated, awkward stab at catching it before it hit the ground. Then he picked it up and trudged back to the gathering players.

Was that his fault or Townsend's? It was a good question, one not easily answered, but Gene was certain there would be more than one player on the team who was sure he already knew the answer.

"Okay, there, Gene!" called Linardi from the sideline. "That's all right. Try it again."

Gene nodded and ducked into the huddle.

"What's the matter, Merrill?" Townsend asked. "You were a little slow on that one."

"Either I was a little slow or you were too soon. Try it again."

"Sure. On three."

This time as Gene went out he kept his eye on Townsend. And as soon as he saw the quarterback's arm go back, he spun about and started back to the line of scrimmage. But Townsend did not release the ball. He waited until Gene was much less than ten yards from the scrimmage line before he rifled the ball.

Gene braced himself as the ball slammed into his chest with the force of a cannon shot. It knocked the breath out of him; and before he could wrap his arms around the ball, it had bounced high into the air for the second time. Again Gene tried—fruitlessly—to catch the ball before it struck the gound.

"I gave you plenty of time, didn't I?" asked a very satisfied Townsend. "Now what's your excuse?"

"I haven't got any," said Gene. "Skip Wittington throws harder than that and I had no trouble with his short passes. I should have caught this one. It was my fault."

"You want to try it again?" Townsend asked, obviously perfectly willing to continue Gene's torment.

"Sure."

This time, as Gene bolted from the line of scrimmage, he kept his eyes straight ahead. Then, instead of waiting until he had covered the full thirteen yards, he spun about after covering only about ten.

Sure enough. Since Townsend was deliberately throwing too soon this time, Gene caught him in the act of releasing the ball. Slowing up, he leaped, caught the ball, tucked it away under his arm, then spun about again for the run downfield. After a few quick, evasive moves, he pulled up and trotted back. He hadn't run a true button hook pattern, but if this was the way Townsend wanted to play it, Gene supposed he could be forgiven for making up his own pass patterns.

This time, as Gene neared the huddle, there was little satisfaction visible on Townsend's face. Nor could Gene help but notice the difficulty a few of the players were having as they tried to suppress their pleasure at Townsend's irritation.

Then, just before Gene reached the huddle, Linardi's whistle shrilled, cutting short the workout. Gene's heart sank. Could Linardi really have seen enough in so short a practice session to make up his mind about Gene fairly?

Well, he'd know soon enough.

4

"SIT DOWN, GENE," Linardi said, closing the door to his office and indicating with a sweep of his hand the wooden chair by his desk.

Gene sat down. He was unhappily aware that Cartwright had just left the coach's office with a pleased look on his face.

Linardi sat down behind his desk and looked Gene over shrewdly for a moment before speaking. "You looked good out there, Gene," he said finally. "Very good, indeed. I'll admit that I was surprised."

"Thanks, Mr. Linardi."

"Call me Coach, Gene. All my players do. You might as well get used to the idea, since I see no reason why you shouldn't start considering yourself a member of the team."

Gene sat suddenly straighter. He wondered for an instant if he had heard correctly. Linardi smiled at his reaction.

"But I just saw Cartwright leaving here," Gene said. "He looked like you'd just told *him* . . ."

"I did. He's going to start the Johnson City game at split end. You'll be warming the bench.

If this school was big enough to have a junior varsity program, you'd be on the junior varsity team. But all we've got is the freshman team, and you're too old for that. So you'll be on the team, but as I said, you'll just be warming the bench."

At the look on Gene's face, Linardi held up his hand and said, "Now don't let that discourage you. You are plenty fast, faster than Cartwright, and you've got great hands. You seem to know the standard pass patterns surprisingly well." He paused and began to fiddle with a yellow pencil he picked up from the blotter. "But that's not enough, Gene. You lack game experience. After all—as I have said before—you've never played a regulation game of football in your life."

What the man was saying was quite true, Gene realized. So where did that leave him?

"You need to go easy at first, Gene. I'll put you in gradually, feed you in, as it were—not when anything crucial is at stake, you understand, only when I can afford whatever mistakes you might make. After that it's up to you. If you can show me that you can handle yourself on a field in game action, I'll let you start—if, that is, Marble is not ready to play by that time."

"That's an awful lot of ifs."

"I know it is. But I'd like to see you give it a try. I know it's not going to be easy for you, but then

I'm sure you realize this from the greeting you got from Townsend and the others today."

Gene nodded grimly.

"All right, then. I'll do what I can for you. And incidentally, I'd like you to know that I saw today a side of Jeff Townsend I never thought existed, which only goes to prove that you really *can't* tell a book from its cover. Nevertheless, Gene, Townsend's my quarterback. He's cool under fire. He knows how to pass and how to pick apart an opposing defense. Furthermore, his skill and cockiness inspire the team. You'll just have to learn to work with him."

Gene nodded. "It doesn't seem too likely, but I'll try."

"Look. You've got one thing going for you—and it's a lot. Jeff Townsend likes to win. We all do. So Townsend's not going to do anything that might endanger his chance of coming out on top, which means that all you've got to do is show him—along with the rest of us—that we can win with you at split end. Do that and you'll have no trouble with Townsend. I guarantee it."

Linardi slapped the pencil down upon the blotter. The interview was over.

Gene stood up to go.

"Here," said the coach, reaching into a drawer and pulling out a loose-leaf notebook. "I've got something for you. Study these plays. Get each pass pattern down so you can run it blindfolded. Then you'll really be able to help us."

As Gene took the notebook, Linardi stood up also and slapped Gene warmly on the back. "And good luck, Gene. I'd like to see you make it. We could use an end with your speed and your hands."

"I'll try," said Gene, as he left the office.

But as he walked home through the clear, late afternoon sunlight, he was not so sure he'd like to bet any money on his chances—especially with Townsend at quarterback.

One day Skip had been discussing with Gene the relationship that had to exist between a good quarterback and his receiver. Skip had likened it to a kind of marriage. Both partners made allowances and tried to understand the other so well that each one got to know instinctively what to expect from the other in almost any given passing situation.

But obviously no such relationship with Townsend was at all likely to develop. He and Gene simply did not go well together, and furthermore . . .

"Golly, Gene, you must have money in the bank," said a familiar voice behind him, "walking along like this talking to yourself."

Gene's heart skipped a beat as he turned quickly. Barbara Collins, her arms full of books, grinned impishly as she caught the surprise on his face.

"I don't go around talking to myself," Gene protested mildly, enormously pleased and grateful at the steadiness in his voice.

"Well, maybe you don't usually, but I've been walking along behind you for a half a block now, and you've been shaking your head at something, and your lips *have* been moving. Sometimes you even wave your hands. I'd say you were having a real debate with yourself."

"Circumstantial evidence," said Gene. "I'm not talking to myself. I'm just having a nervous breakdown."

"Better if you had money in the bank."

"No such luck, I'm afraid."

Gene moved over to allow Barbara to walk along beside him. Then he realized that this put him on the inside with her on the outside. Quickly he stopped and stepped to her other side. "Not polite," he mumbled. "Girl should always walk on the inside."

"Yes," she said, smiling up at him. "That's the way I like it, too. Makes me feel protected."

Gene felt his face redden, while his heart continued the wild, foolish thumping it had begun the minute Barbara's voice had broken into his thoughts. He didn't know whether to be pleased with Barbara for upsetting him like this—or angry. He felt so vulnerable all of a sudden. It astonished him that such a simple thing as a girl walking beside him could have this kind of an effect on him—especially Barbara Collins, a girl he had known practically all his life.

But no, he thought as he glanced quickly down at her. He hadn't really known her all his life—not *this* Barbara Collins. Something incredible had happened to her over the past two summers, something close to magic—and almost as frightening. He'd watched the transformation from a distance, amazed and troubled and vaguely anxious. When he'd seen her entering the Roxy with Paul Marble this past summer, the sight had so upset him that for the rest of the summer, at odd moments when he'd least expect it, he would recall the two of them entering the theater and a feeling close to panic would sweep over him.

And now Barbara was walking beside him.

"Gene, aren't you playing on the football team now?"

Gene patted the notebook Coach Linardi had given him. "Looks like it."

"Was it because of that catch you made the other day?"

"I guess in a way it was."

"Poor Paul. He's afraid that knee of his will keep him out for the rest of the season."

"It's his own fault."

"I know, Gene," she said gently. "He told me

all about it. They thought they'd teach you a lesson. They ended up teaching themselves a lesson. You weren't hurt at all, huh?"

"Nope."

"But you haven't played much football, have you? How did you learn to catch like that?"

"I've been practicing since last spring with Skip Wittington. He was hurt pretty bad and came home to recuperate. Soon as he could hobble around, we began working out. He's a great passer, Barbara. If his knee holds up, he should really make history at State."

She frowned up at him. "Skip Wittington?"

"That's right. You remember Skip. He was only the best quarterback Pine Ridge ever had, that's all."

She nodded, her frown gradually fading. Then she tossed back her blond curls with a quick snap of her head. "I know you and Townsend don't get along, Gene, but he's not exactly a flop at quarterback. I'll bet he'll be as good as Skip was."

"Maybe, but this is his first full season. We'll see when it's over."

"I suppose you got to know Skip pretty well."

"Yes, I guess I did. He's a real great guy."

She looked up at him again, seemed about to say something, then looked away. "I'm sure he is, Gene."

"And he really taught me a lot. If I ever do anything at split end this year, it'll be on account of what he taught me."

"But—what about your leg? Will that be all right?"

If anyone else other than Barbara had brought it up, he would have been angry. But Barbara's interest only seemed to warm him; he felt no resentment at all. "Sure, it'll be all right," he replied. "The doctor told me and my folks a long time ago that my right leg will always be somewhat weaker than the other one. But outside of that there's nothing wrong with it—except for the fact that it's a little shorter than the other. While I had polio, it just stopped growing for a while. That's why I limp."

"I hardly notice it at all, Gene."

There was nothing she could have said that would have pleased him more than that. He did not trust himself to make a reply. Instead, he just reached over and gently took from her the load of books she was carrying.

"Your father wants to speak to you," Gene's mother informed him as soon as he entered the house.

Gene was a little surprised at her tone. Dropping onto the hall table the notebook Linardi had given him, he looked at her closely. She was standing in the living room doorway, a white towel wrapped nun-like around her head, a smudge of flour, as usual, showing on her right cheek. She seemed uneasy.

"What's up, Ma?"

"Just go in and see him. He's been waiting in his room for you."

Gene walked through the bedroom into the small study beyond. Once it had been a little back porch. But when his father became the station-master, he had decided he needed a room of his own for working on timetables and freight and rate schedules.

Now he was sitting in the battered old wingback easy chair in the corner close to the one window. He was barely visible in the dimness, his face like a pale flower in the darkness of the chair. He leaned forward and took the unlighted pipe from his mouth as Gene entered the room.

"Sit down, Gene. I've been waiting for you to get home. You're usually home by the three-ten express, aren't you?"

Then he frowned and reached into his vest pocket for his massive gold watch. He consulted it, seemed to recall something important, then looked back up at Gene. He shook his head and smiled. "Foolish of me. The three-ten doesn't go through any more, does it."

"No, Dad. It doesn't."

As his father slowly put away his watch, Gene said, "I'm home late because I was practicing with the football team." He found it difficult to keep the excitement out of his voice. "I was issued a uniform today. I'm officially on the team—split end."

Mr. Merrill's eyebrows went up at the announcement, and he seemed to snap back into the present. His eyes grew more alert. He leaned forward. "I thought you had decided not to go out for the team. That's what you told your mother when you got home last night."

"I changed my mind, Dad. It was a letter from Skip that helped me change it. And I'm glad now that I did. I think I might make the team as a regular."

His father nodded. "All right. But that's not what I wanted to see you about. It's this business with you and Skip. You've gone ahead and gotten yourself too thick with that boy. Now your mother tells me we're expected to go with you and the Wittingtons to the Alfred Tech game in Hamilton. That right?"

"Sure, Dad. What's wrong with that? I thought you liked the Wittingtons."

"Of course I do, Gene. But why can't they ride in their own car?"

"You know why, Dad. They still have that old Ford. Would *you* drive a hundred miles in that?"

"Well, why doesn't Fred get a new car then?"

"I understand he's planning to do just that—as soon as he finds out about that bakery. Golly, Dad, what's wrong with us taking them? We've got plenty of room in that big Oldsmobile of ours—and we hardly *ever* use it."

Mr. Merrill sighed and shook his head in exasperation. "Listen, Gene. It isn't that I'm prejudiced. It's just that I don't want people talking, that's all. This is a small town. There's no sense in getting the neighbors all riled up. You know what they'd say if we drove off with the Wittingtons. And that wouldn't be good for you *or* the Wittingtons. And don't forget, Gene, this is your hometown, too. You've got to live here and go to school here."

"You don't want to go with them because people in town would talk."

"Well, of course they would, Gene."

"What about going into business with Fred—managing that bakery for him? You seemed serious enough when you talked to him about that."

"But of course I *wasn't*, Gene. You should have known that. I just didn't want him to think—well, you know."

"That you were prejudiced."

"No, Gene! Not prejudiced. Just realistic. It wouldn't work out, that's all."

"Okay, Dad."

Mr. Merrill leaned back. "So you see, Gene. It's out of the question for your mother and me to go to Hamilton with the Wittingtons."

"Of course, Dad, if that's the way you feel."

"Well, that certainly is sensible, Gene." He looked past Gene at his wife standing in the doorway. "You see, Martha? I told you Gene would be sensible."

Gene cleared his throat. "But you won't mind if I go with the Wittingtons, will you, Dad?"

"Well now let's think a minute, Son. Wouldn't that be as bad as if *we* went with the Wittingtons?"

"Yes, I suppose it would." Gene paused a moment, as if to consider this new element. "All right, then. If the tickets come, I'll send them back to Skip and tell him that I can't go to the game with him. How's that?"

Mr. Merrill nodded. "Good idea."

"All right, Dad. And while I'm about it, I'll just explain to him about the neighbors and how people would talk. I know Skip will understand. I've talked to him lots of times about the people in this town, and he knows them pretty well."

Mr. Merrill suddenly leaned forward in his chair. "Well, now, wait just a minute, Gene. There's no need for you to mention anything like that at all."

"Dad, I've already told Bill we're going with them if Skip sends the tickets. They've got to have some explanation if we don't go with them—and of course they'll know even if we don't tell them. So I'd rather be the one to tell them. Then there'd be no misunderstandings, Dad. Then they'd know where they stand with us. We would then be just as honest with them as the other people in town who don't make any effort to hide the way they feel. It's the only fair thing to do, Dad."

Gene's mother said softly to her husband, "Ralph, I think that we should let Gene go to the football game with the Wittingtons. And perhaps we should go along, too. And during the drive, you can explain to Fred why you don't think this town needs a bakery—at least one managed by you. You've got to tell him sometime. I understand he's already inquired into the price of the old bakery on Market Street."

Gene's father shook his head wearily. "Okay," he said unhappily, "but don't say I didn't warn you. There's no telling where this will all end."

"We don't have to make a big fuss about it, Ralph. We'll just get into the car and drive off like anyone else would."

"What about the neighbors, Martha? Some rubberneck's sure to see us."

"I guess," said Gene's mother, "that it's time we realized that the Wittingtons are our neighbors, too."

Later that evening after supper, in the privacy of his room, Gene opened the notebook Coach Linardi had given him and tried to concentrate on the diagrammed plays. Unfortunately, he couldn't make too much sense out of the dotted lines, the inverted v's, the flow charts, and all of the other special symbols used by the coach to indicate what each formation meant and how it should be developed.

Gene gave up at length and rolled over onto his back on the bed and stared up at the crazy crack in the ceiling—the one that sometimes looked like a man running, or at other times resembled the face of a hound. Only now he didn't see the crack. He saw instead Barbara Collins and the way she tipped her head when she turned to look up at him—and the quick way she had of tossing her hair back over her shoulder.

It had been some day. He had taken so many steps this day, had opened so many doors. The only thing was—could he keep them all open? Could he really make the team? Would it be all right when the Wittingtons and his parents went to Hamilton together? And would he be able to walk home with Barbara Collins again?

The prospect lit a fire within him, and his thoughts raced ahead to the next day. At last reality asserted itself. Gene sighed, rolled over, and went back to puzzling over the play book. Gradually the diagrams began to make sense.

He was still at it when his mother came up around eleven o'clock to suggest he turn off his light and get some sleep.

5

GENE STOOD UP and tried to get his helmet to settle more easily down over his ears. As he did so, an ominous quiet fell over those players nearest him. Without looking around, Gene could feel their eyes on him. They still could not believe it—Gene Merrill was wearing the maroon-and-gold uniform of the Pine Ridge Hornets.

Wendell Huff, on his way out to the field, paused in front of Gene. The big Negro's face broke into a sudden smile. "What's the matter, Merrill? Didn't you know how big your ears were?"

Gene shook his head in frustration. "It just feels so uncomfortable—like I'm in a deep sea diver's helmet."

"Forget how it feels. You'll get used to it. And the first time it comes between your head and a tackler's knee, you'll never feel uncomfortable in it again."

"Maybe," said Gene as he took off the helmet and followed Huff from the locker room.

Gene was halfway to the bench when he heard his name called. He glanced to his right and saw Barbara Collins running out with the rest of the cheer leaders. Dressed in her maroon-and-gold short skirt and white bulky-knit sweater, she looked very pretty.

He waved and she waved back.

"Good luck!" she called.

"You'll need more than luck, Merrill."

Gene turned to see Townsend pulling up beside him.

"You may think that uniform feels funny on you," Townsend went on, "but you have no idea how funny it looks on you."

With that parting shot, Townsend started to trot toward the bench; but Gene overtook him easily.

"Why don't you just wait and see what happens in a game?" Gene demanded. "If I do happen to find myself out there with you at quarterback, you're going to want me to play hard and to run hard. So why don't you just try to forget how much we dislike each other and concentrate on playing football?"

Townsend pulled up; Gene stopped running also. "Okay, then," Townsend replied. "You surprise me, Merrill. You sound very sensible. But just make sure you *do* concentrate on playing football—and not on the cheerleaders. And forget any fancy notions you might have about being a hero. You're going to have to be a lot tougher than I know you are to last out on that playing field."

"Forget the lectures, Townsend. I like Linardi's better. You throw the ball and I'll catch it. That's all you have to worry about."

Before Townsend could reply, Gene turned and left him, heading for the bench.

When he slumped down beside Jim Martin a moment later, Jim took one look at him and said, "What's the matter with you? You look like you're ready to chew this bench up and spit it out."

"Not this *bench,* Jim," Gene said bitterly. "Someone on it."

"Could that someone be a certain quarterback?"

Gene looked at Jim. "Could be."

"Don't see how I can blame you. I feel just the way you do about that showboat. Pretty Boy, that's what I call him."

Just then Linardi waved to those players on the bench, and each one promptly scrambled toward him to hear the man's last minute instructions and game assignments. Their opposition—the Westfield Tornadoes—had just finished running through some drills on the field and were now trotting off the field toward their bench on the other side.

As Gene pulled up just outside the crowd of players surrounding Linardi, he could not help glancing back to see if he could catch a glimpse of Barbara. He saw her in front of the stands—a huge maroon megaphone in one hand—talking quite animatedly with another cheerleader. She did not see him. He turned back and tried to catch the coach's words. Townsend was right. He should concentrate on football, not on the cheerleaders.

Cartwright started the game. He did fine; so well, in fact, that Gene felt, along with only a mild tinge of disappointment, a definite feeling of relief. Townsend and the rest of the team, it seemed, had worried themselves to no end, for Gene Merrill was not likely to see much action this season as a member of their precious team. Cartwright could obviously do it all, despite his lack of speed.

After an unfortunate first quarter, during which Townsend experienced some difficulty in getting the team's offense coordinated, the team finally began to move the ball downfield, as Townsend, exploiting a weakness in the left side of the Tornado line, sent Ketchel and Huff through it, over it, and around it—almost invariably for sizable gains.

Then, as soon as the Westfield linebackers and linemen swung their attention to that side of the line, Townsend opened up on the right side. Short line plunges, end-arounds, and one particularly damaging pass to Cartwright put the Hornets on the Tornado five-yard line with a first and ten.

A fake to the right half with Huff crashing over left tackle brought them two yards closer to the end zone. But then a fancy reverse lost three yards. Dolph Linardi started to pace up and down the sideline in front of the bench. He needn't have worried. On the next play Townsend sent Cartwright into the end zone and hit him chest high for the score.

Townsend had made it look easy as he faked a handoff to Ketchel up the middle, then drifted back and shot the ball on a line to Cartwright. Toward the end of the second quarter, Townsend got the team moving again and went all the way a second time to makes it fourteen to nothing.

Despite himself, Gene felt a grudging respect for Townsend, a respect that grew not only as a result of what he saw but by what Jim Martin failed to see, for Gene found that almost without exception everything Jim Martin predicted failed to come about. Whenever Jim muttered that Townsend would have to pass, Gene could be pretty certain that Townsend would not pass. Time after time Townsend chose plays absolutely contrary to those Jim Martin predicted. Yet the team continued to move with crunching effectiveness over its opposition. It was on its way to still another score when the gun sounded, ending the first half.

Soon after the second half commenced, however, it became apparent to Gene along with everyone else that the Westfield coach had made quite a few angry noises during half time. On the first play from scrimmage after the kickoff, Townsend tried a reverse. Two Tornado tacklers hit Terry Lowden with such fury that the little halfback lost the ball. A Westfield linebacker snatched up the tumbling football and galloped the short twenty yards into the Pine Ridge end zone.

Depressingly soon thereafter, a Townsend pass was picked off by a Westfield defensive back. Before the dust had cleared, the Tornadoes had scored a second time to tie it all up.

For the rest of that quarter, the two teams slugged it out toe to toe, with neither side gaining any significant yardage and each team's punter seeing lots of action. What had looked like a runaway victory for Pine Ridge in the first half had become a bruising defensive slugging match in the second.

Then Townsend got the Hornets moving again. A big gain by Wendell Huff on a delayed trap up the middle sparked the offense, and Ketchel kept the pot boiling as he steamrolled around the left side of the Westfield line to put the ball on their forty.

With a first and ten Townsend surprised everyone by passing to Billy Hutchins, his left end. He sent him on a quick slant over the middle. It was a good call and Hutchins made a fine grab as he leaped high into the air for the ball. But before he could come down with the ball, a green-and-white clad tackler busted into him from behind.

Gene groaned when he saw how Hutchins hit the ground. He landed face down and stayed that way, his body absolutely still. Gene jumped to his feet as a group of anxious Pine Ridge players surrounded the ominously quiet form. Linardi and the school doctor hurried out onto the field. But a moment later, to Gene's relief, Hutchins was sitting up. The anxious circle of players dispersed, and two burly defensive players helped the end off the field. Just ahead of them came Linardi, heading directly toward Gene.

"Merrill!" he called. "Get out here! You're taking Cartwright's position at right end. He'll fill in for Billy."

Gene jumped to his feet stunned. Then he began looking for his helmet. Someone found it under the bench and thrust it toward him. He grabbed it and raced out onto the field.

Townsend was waiting for him as Gene—still fumbling with his helmet's chin strap—approached the huddle. "You better get that helmet on, Merrill. These guys are playing football out here."

Gene said nothing as he ducked into the huddle. One glance around at the grim faces told him just how intent each player was on keeping this drive alive.

"I'm going to use you right away, Cartwright,"

Townsend announced. "Their defense probably figures you for a dummy that doesn't know Billy's patterns. So the next play—naturally—is going to be another quick slant over the middle. Got it?"

Cartwright nodded.

"Okay. On four, you guys, and let's see some execution."

As Gene trotted over to his position, he reviewed his own assignment. On any pass to the left end, he was to run a quick slant through the flat, then cut straight downfield to clear out the area. Certain he knew his assignment, he waited—as tight as a bow string—for the snap.

When it came he launched himself forward, his cleats digging cleanly into the ground with each stride. Beyond the scrimmage line he cut to his left into the flat. But he never reached it. The Westfield linebacker slipped sideways and launched himself at Gene with devastating precision. Gene tried to swerve away, but the linebacker cut both legs out from under him. The sky and earth exchanged places as Gene slammed to the ground. Only dimly was he aware of the linebacker scrambling to his feet and starting downfield after Cartwright.

Gene shook the cobwebs out of his head and watched as Cartwright, the ball now safely tucked away, broke a tackle and dug for yardage. He made at least five more yards before a gang of tacklers pulled him down.

Gene got to his feet and headed back for the huddle. A lot of help *he'd* been.

"Did you have a nice rest, Merrill?" Townsend inquired as Gene ducked into the huddle.

"Well, at least I kept that linebacker busy."

"Sure you did. Except that he was the one who finally helped pull down Cartwright."

Gene just kept his head down and waited for Townsend to call the next play.

The completed pass to Cartwright had been good for another first down and put them on Westfield's thirty-yard line. Townsend then called on Ketchel for a slant over left tackle. But the fullback got nowhere. On the next play Huff tried to sweep right end and lost six yards, to make it third and fourteen.

On each play Gene's assignment had been to hightail it downfield to help clear out the secondary. He had failed completely, however, as the Westfield linebacker continued to dump him with almost insolent ease. On this last play, he had been flattened again.

How could he catch a pass, Gene wondered miserably, as he trudged back to the huddle, if he couldn't even get past the line of scrimmage?

Townsend was on one knee as the huddle closed about him. "They know we have to pass, but there's not much else we can do with third and fourteen. So we'll go with a play action pass. Run a post, Cartwright, and don't look for the ball until you're in the corner." Townsend looked at his little scatback. "Terry, run a slant in over the middle. If Cartwright's covered, I'll have to go to you."

Glancing quickly across the huddle at Gene, Townsend said, "And if you think you can tear yourself away from that linebacker friend of yours, Merrill, run a cross-over to the other corner of the end zone. If worse comes to worse, I might even have to throw to you." Despite their weariness, almost everyone in the huddle broke into a grin.

Then Townsend looked at Ketchel. "The fake'll be to you, Seth. Old number three—right up the middle. Make it look good." He glanced quickly around the huddle. "On set. Let's go all the way on this one, fellows. It just might be our last chance."

As Gene headed for his position, Townsend's words kept sounding in his ears. *That linebacker friend of yours.* Townsend, it seemed, had not missed a thing; he and the rest of the team were simply amused at Gene's hapless attempts to play football.

Furious, Gene went down on his three-point stance and tried to keep his face blank. It was not easy, considering the way he felt. Across the line of scrimmage his nemesis was also crouching.

Gene thought he caught the faint trace of a smirk on the big fellow's broad face.

Townsend bent over the center and called set. The ball slapped up into his waiting palms as both lines exploded. Rising from his stance, Gene headed across the line of scrimmage, directly at the linebacker. The fellow saw him coming and grinned. A front tooth, Gene noticed, was missing. Abruptly Gene swerved to the outside. The linebacker cut over to head Gene off; but as soon as he did, Gene spun around and darted to the inside.

The linebacker turned back and tried desperately to grab Gene, but by that time Gene was past him. As Gene crossed into the end zone a second or two later, he saw the Tornado deep safety hustling over to cover him. Gene slowed almost to a halt and the safety appeared to relax. At once Gene poured it on and swept past him. Alone in the end zone, he looked back.

His heart almost stopped. The football was in the air and heading directly for him! It was coming shoulder high, fast and true, like a hundred other passes Skip Wittington had thrown to him that past summer. At the thought of Skip, Gene felt the tension fall away from him. He reached out almost casually and caught the football.

Touchdown!

As he trotted back to the huddle, Gene had all he could do to keep a grin off his face.

"Nice going," Terry Lowden said.

"Yeah, Gene, a fine catch," said Huff.

"That's right," said Townsend coldly. "That was a nice catch."

"Well, your pass was right on the button," Gene replied. "Couldn't have been any better."

Townsend ignored Gene's response and quietly gave the signals for the point-after kick.

It was a good one and the Hornets went ahead, twenty-one to fourteen. There was no more scoring for either team after that. The Westfield linebacker—evidently furious with himself for his costly lapse—continued his private war with Gene so effectively that Gene caught no more passes that afternoon. Nevertheless, when the final gun sounded, Gene was a very happy player as he limped proudly off the field.

He was bone-weary. Every muscle in his body was chorusing its protest. But the team had won, and he had helped. A celebration was in order, and already he had made up his mind to ask Barbara Collins for a date that night.

And the way he felt, he wouldn't take no for an answer.

6

GENE HAD HOPED that Barbara would be all ready to go the moment he reached her house. That way he wouldn't have to go inside, just stand on the porch and wait for Barbara to slip into her coat.

Barbara's younger sister opened the door. "Yes?" She was a bright-faced little urchin with an auburn pony tail and was wearing a red corduroy jumper with a white frilly blouse. She could not have been more than eight years old.

Gene cleared his throat. "Is Barbara ready yet? We're going to the show."

"Oh, you're Barbara's date!" She stepped back into the hallway and turned her head. "He's here, Bobby! Your date's here!"

Then she looked back at Gene. "You better come in and wait. She's not near ready yet."

Gene squared his shoulders and stepped into the house.

"I'm Judy," she said as she closed the door. "Come on into the living room and wait."

Gene followed Judy into the living room, sighted a sofa by the far wall, and headed toward it. The moment he sat down, however, Barbara's parents entered the room, quizzical smiles on their faces. Gene got hastily to his feet.

"You must be Gene Merrill," Mr. Collins said, extending his hand.

Gene shook the man's hand and nodded. "Yes-sir, I'm Gene Merrill."

Barbara's father then introduced him to Mrs. Collins. She smiled at Gene, then sat down in a soft chair. "I understand you play on the high school football team, Gene," she said.

"Yes, that's right. I do."

"You play end, is that it?" asked Barbara's father, making himself comfortable in another soft chair.

Gene sat back down on the sofa. "Yes, I play end. We had our first game today."

"And you won, I believe."

"How do you feel after today's game?"

"Sore," Gene replied honestly. "All over."

Mr. Collins laughed. "I can believe that. Football's a rough game. Do you like it?"

"Yes. Very much. I'm sort of new at it, as a matter of fact. But I do like to play."

"Yes, so Barbara told us at dinner." Mrs. Collins frowned. "Is it *your* mother who bakes those delicious cakes?"

"Yes, it is."

Mrs. Collins glanced at her husband, then looked back at Gene. "Your mother is some cook—a Ma Merrill cake is really something."

"Thank you, Mrs. Collins. Most people do seem to like them. And I know Ma uses only the very best ingredients."

"I'm sure she does," Mrs. Collins said. "You must be very proud."

"Yes, I am."

"Your father used to be stationmaster here in town, didn't he?" Mr. Collins asked, offering Gene a cigarette.

Gene refused the cigarette with a quick shake of his head. "That's right, Mr. Collins. He used to be. But he's retired now."

Mrs. Collins frowned slightly. "Barbara should be down soon," she said. "I'm sure I don't know what's keeping her."

Mr. Collins smiled at Gene. "Unfortunately, Gene, you'd better start getting used to waiting for females. It's the way you're going to spend a good deal of your allotted time on this planet."

Gene smiled. Barbara's parents didn't seem so bad, and he seemed to have passed the inspection himself. Of course, it wasn't over yet.

Abruptly Mrs. Collins got up from her chair, patted her husband on the shoulder, and left the room, explaining that she was expecting some guests later that evening.

Mr. Collins put the cigarette he had offered Gene into his mouth and lit it. "Do you drive a car, Gene?"

"I can drive, Mr. Collins, but I don't have a car. My father says the insurance is too high for kids my age."

"It is high, of course—and for good reason. Well, I'm glad you're not one of those hot-rod enthusiasts. Sometimes I wish Barbara didn't drive."

Quick but light footsteps on the main stairway caused both of them to turn. Barbara swirled into the living room. "Hi, Gene. I'm ready!"

Gene got to his feet, confused. Barbara was so beautiful he felt dazzled, unfairly so.

"Well," Mr. Collins said, getting up and snubbing out his cigarette, "you two have a good time." He smiled at Gene. "Get her back here at a decent hour, Gene. Twelve at the latest."

"Yes, Mr. Collins."

Outside on the porch Gene stopped and looked at Barbara. "Wow! I'm glad that's over."

"Was meeting the folks so awful, Gene?"

"No, it wasn't awful. Not much awful. You came down just in time, I think. And boy, you really do look nice."

"Thank you; Gene."

"No, I'm wrong. You don't look nice. You look beautiful. Maybe even too beautiful to be going out with a guy like me."

"Don't talk nonsense, Gene. I've been waiting for you to ask me out since we were in the sixth grade."

She laughed at the look on his face and grabbed his elbow. "Come on. It's a long walk to the movies, and I don't want to miss the cartoons."

The only thing wrong with the walk to the movies was that they eventually got there. As far as Gene was concerned, it could have—and should have—gone on forever. The next time, he promised himself when they reached the theater, he'd just ask her for a date and not mention the movies. Then they'd spend the date just walking around and talking.

The movie—a Walt Disney affair—was at best an irksome interruption. As soon as it was over, Gene hurried Barbara out of the theater.

"Brrr!" Barbara said, snuggling into her short coat. "It's chilly out."

"Summer is going, all right. I hate the fall and I hate the winter," Gene said, taking her arm and directing her toward the drugstore on the corner. "To me, this is when the old year ends and the new one begins. Not sometime in the middle of winter just after Christmas."

Barbara smiled. "I know what you mean. New

school year. New teachers. New courses. New fall outfits. And summer romances dead or dying."

"What's that about summer romances?" Gene asked, as lightly as he could.

"Oh, you know what I mean," she replied, laughing mischievously.

Gene stepped ahead of her and pulled open the drugstore's door for her. As she stepped past him into the store, he said, "No, I *don't* know what you mean."

"Well, then. Forget it. The romance is dead. Kaput. Finished. Remember what we said. This is the time for new teachers, new courses, new fall outfits—and new romances—I hope."

Gene knew what she meant, all right. It was clear enough to send his pulse rate soaring. But he was a big boy now, he told himself, so he wasn't going to start jumping into the air and clicking his heels—even if that was what he felt like doing.

He helped her carefully off with her coat, then slid into the booth across from her. It was the first time that evening he'd really had a chance to look at her.

What he saw was a very pretty girl with straw-colored hair worn long enough to reach her shoulders, brown eyes, a small, perky nose and a light sprinkling of freckles across the bridge of the nose and above her lightly-tanned cheeks. Her lips were full, and she had not painted them with that crazy white stuff some of the girls were using.

"You said something earlier," Gene said. "Something about wanting to go out with me since the sixth grade. Were you pulling my leg?"

"I wouldn't dream of doing such a thing, Gene."

"Okay, then, will you please tell me one thing?"

"What's that?"

"Why the heck didn't you let me *know?*"

She laughed. "That wouldn't have been proper."

The waitress stopped at their booth to see what they wanted. They both ordered chocolate shakes.

As the waitress left, Gene leaned forward. "Come on, why didn't you let me know?"

"Well . . ." she frowned. "You changed so much after your sickness. It *was* polio, wasn't it?"

"That's right. Polio. But what do you mean I changed? My limp?"

"No, not that, Gene. That's hardly noticeable at all. I mean *you* changed. You sort of forgot how to smile, and you withdrew from things."

"You mean I became less active. I was told to, Barbara—the doctor, my folks, everyone. All of a sudden I found myself being careful of everything, I guess."

"Even of people, Gene?"

"I guess so. I guess that, too. But that was so

long ago. How come you remember so far back?"

"I remember lots of things, Gene. And don't forget, when the elementary school was on Elm Street, you used to walk right past my house on the way to school."

He smiled. "I remember. There was a big dog on the corner. It looked as big as a mountain to me."

"It should have. It was a Great Dane."

"And you were afraid to go past it."

"Unless you took me."

Gene smiled. Yes, he remembered. He had dreaded going by that dog, but he had always managed somehow to fight back his fear and escort Barbara past the monstrous, slavering animal. Gene realized now that the dog had only been trying to be friendly; but whenever it came bounding down off the porch toward them, Gene's knees turned to water. He would hold out his hand to ward off the dog's charge, while over and over in a small, frightened voice he would call, *Nice doggy. Nice doggy.*

"You were so brave," Barbara said.

"I was petrified. The only reason I didn't turn tail and run myself was I didn't want to look chicken in front of a girl."

The waitress brought their shakes.

"Anyway, you got me past it all right. You were my brave knight." She pulled her milkshake toward her and took the straws from their wrapper. "You have no idea how glad I was when the family that owned the dog moved off the block."

Gene grinned suddenly. "It was about that time, I think, that I discovered just how awful little girls were. Some kids in my class made me want to curl up and die when they suggested I was in love with you."

She laughed, delighted. "You poor guy. No wonder you just sort of vanished."

Gene laughed also and turned his attention back to his own milkshake. It was startling how much he remembered, and how much Barbara remembered as well. He stole a glance at her. She had grown so and was as different from that little skinny kid with the stringy blonde hair as he was from that little boy who had to run everywhere and who climbed trees and was always the longest one to stay inside the ring in dodge ball. That wiry little boy was gone forever, and so was that little blonde girl with the white, milky face and the pleading eyes. He might not be overjoyed at what he had become, but he sure couldn't complain about Barbara's transformation.

"Well," he said, "now we're almost grown up."

Barbara looked up from her milkshake. "Are you going to college, Gene?"

"I don't think so. I'd need a scholarship, and I'm not that bright."

She frowned slightly. "Jeff Townsend's already heard from a couple of colleges."

"Football scholarships?"

"That's right, Gene. Since you're on the team now, couldn't you get one too?"

"Just being on the team isn't enough, Barbara. You have to be good—real good."

"You'll get better, Gene. You did fine today."

"Perhaps. But I sure had some difficulty getting past the line of scrimmage. Westfield had a linebacker that really gave me fits."

"You'll catch on."

"Sure. But I'll never be a Jeff Townsend, and that's what it takes to get a football scholarship. No, college is out for me, Barbara. My father's pension from the Pennsy and Southern is a good one, and pretty soon he'll be eligible for Social Security. But that's not enough to put me through college."

"Well, what are you going to do?"

"I've been thinking of joining the Navy and letting them teach me a trade. I'm interested in electronics."

She wrinkled her nose.

"I know it doesn't sound very romantic," he said. "College *would* be nice. But it's not for me, that's all."

"You shouldn't go striking yourself out so soon."

"I'm not striking myself out. I'm just being realistic."

She smiled. "Well, I've got a feeling that before you leave high school, you'll discover something about yourself—that for you being realistic means setting your sights a lot higher than the Navy."

Gene shrugged, a little taken aback by her alarming confidence in him. "Well, I sure would like to think you're right. Could be. Look at Skip Wittington. He's doing great at State. Not only on the football field, but also in the class room. He's majoring in psychology—clinical psychology." Gene shook his head in admiration. "Of course, he's smart enough to do anything he wants, I guess. I don't suppose he ever had his sights set any lower than what they are now."

Barbara was frowning. "You think a lot of Skip, don't you."

"Sure."

"Well, I think you're overestimating him, Gene."

"Why do you say that?"

"You praise him to the skies, then downgrade yourself."

"No, I don't. I just happen to like the guy, that's all. If I ever do make it good on the team, it'll be because he worked out with me so much this past summer."

"No, it won't. It'll be because you helped him

by working out with him so he could get back into shape. That was why you did it, wasn't it?"

"Well yes, it was."

"Of course it was. You don't owe Skip Wittington anything. He owes you a lot for working out with him day after day the way you did."

There was a note in Barbara's voice that alerted Gene. She was obviously angry at something—or someone. "What have you got against Skip, Barbara?"

His question seemed to bother her. "Nothing, Gene. Nothing at all. I'm just trying to keep things straight, that's all."

"Okay, then. Let's keep things straight. I like Skip. He's a great guy, a fine football player, and an excellent student. Now what's *that* got to do with me?"

She sighed. "It's just that I don't want you to sell yourself short by comparing yourself unfavorably with Skip. You helped win a football game today, and I think that makes you pretty good. Even Jeff told me that if it hadn't been for your grab in the end zone, the team might have lost. He said you executed a very neat stunt to get away from that linebacker that had been bothering you. So all I'm saying is that it's time for Gene Merrill to come out of his cocoon."

Gene started to reply, then stopped. He felt uneasy. He had the feeling that Barbara was taking charge a little too swiftly. She was telling him too much about himself, and he didn't like it. She was crowding him.

"Why the frown, Gene?"

"Oh? Was I frowning?"

"Just a slight one. Something I said?"

"No, of course not, Barbara. Look, let's talk about something else. Okay?"

"Of course."

"So tell me, how would you like to see the Alfred Tech-State game?"

Her eyes widened. "You mean you've got tickets?"

"I've got a promise of them, and the game is being played in Hamilton this year. It's not more than a couple of hours from here. My father's driving."

"Sounds wonderful, Gene."

"Then it's a date?"

"Of course, Gene. I'd *love* to go. I really would."

"We'll all be going together, the Wittingtons and us."

"The Wittingtons?"

Barbara had been unable to keep the dismay out of her voice, and something inside Gene collapsed. He had deliberately withheld the Wittingtons' connection with the game until this moment. He had wanted to find out something—and he had.

"That's right," he said. "Skip's the one sending the tickets."

"We're all going together—in one car?"

"There's plenty of room in Dad's car. On the way back, maybe Dad will let me drive."

"Well, why can't the Wittingtons use their own car?"

"It's too old for the trip. That's a hundred miles at least, and Dad's Oldsmobile is in great shape. He hardly ever uses it, and like I said, it's got plenty of room."

She looked down at her milkshake, poked at it with her straws, then looked back up at him, her face surprisingly grim. "I guess not, Gene. I guess I don't want to go after all."

"You mind explaining why not?"

"Just forget it, Gene. It needn't concern us any more. We'll just forget all about it."

Someone put a quarter in the juke box. The sudden blaring beat of the juke box music seemed totally out of keeping with Gene's unhappy thoughts. "It would be nice," he said, "if we *could* just forget. But I don't think we can. It's too important."

"To you, perhaps. But not to me."

"Barbara, what's wrong with you?"

"There's nothing wrong with me. It's you. You and your eagerness to prove something—how noble and how—well, how liberal you are."

"That's not it at all."

"Oh, yes, it is. I can see the accusation in your eyes, and I can hear it in your voice. Just because I don't want to drive all the way to Hamilton with the Wittingtons, there's something wrong with me."

"Well, what's wrong with driving to Hamilton with the Wittingtons?"

"If you don't know, then it would be useless for me to tell you."

"You mean we'd be too crowded," he said with cold sarcasm. When she didn't reply, he bore in relentlessly. "I guess you *don't* have to draw me a picture, Barbara. I understand." He felt his shoulders slump. "I understand perfectly."

Carefully placing her milkshake glass to one side, Barbara leaned forward. In a hard, level voice she said, "You're disappointed in me. I can tell. Well, you really don't understand. You think you do, but you don't."

"All right. I don't understand." Gene glanced up at the blaring ceiling speaker just beside their booth. "Come on. I'll walk you home."

He counted out seventy-five cents, left it on the table, and slid out of the booth. Barbara followed. He helped her silently into her coat, then led the way to the door.

The walk back to her house was a bitter experience. Barbara said nothing—absolutely nothing;

and all during it Gene could not help but contrast this painful silent walk back with the other one they had taken earlier that same evening.

He didn't want the date to end this way. He knew that if it did, there would never be another one. But though he cleared his throat to speak more than once, he could not get a single word to come out. And with each step they took, the harsh silence between them became more solid, more formidable. By the time they reached her house, he had given up.

He mounted the porch steps and went as far as the door with her.

"Goodnight, Gene," she said politely. "I just loved the picture. Thanks for inviting me."

Then she was through the door, and Gene found himself with nothing to do but turn and go home.

As he descended the porch steps and started down Pleasant Street, he told himself that it was a good thing he had found out about her. She was prejudiced—beautiful but prejudiced. She was something that had looked breathtakingly lovely from a distance. But once he had gotten close enough, he had seen the ugliness.

That was what he told himself. But it did no good as far as quieting the ache that grew within him—no good at all.

7

THE HORNETS WERE playing the Fulton Warriors, a team that had not been counted on to give the Hornets much trouble. But the Warriors hadn't read the script, it seemed, and were giving the Hornets a great deal of trouble after all. The name of the trouble was "ball control."

Billy Hutchins was back in at the left-end slot with Cartwright playing back at right end. This put Gene on the bench, watching unhappily as the Fulton Warriors took the ball on their own fourteen-yard line after forcing a punt and started a slow, unspectacular march upfield.

Gene was impressed. There were no long runs, no long passes. Three times they elected to run the ball on fourth down, on each occasion eking out the precious yardage needed for the first down. And so it went until, by the end of the first quarter, with fourth down and goal to go just two yards out, the quarterback kept the ball and burrowed into his line for the touchdown.

It was an example of hard, slogging, basic football, and in the second quarter, after again forcing the Hornets to punt, they started the whole grueling business over again. Exhibiting the same relentless drive, they managed to claw their way steadily downfield to the Hornet goal line, where again a desperate line plunge on fourth down brought them their reward.

This time, however, the Hornets managed to block the kick for the point after.

It was catch-up football after that, but before Townsend could get any kind of a drive going, the gun sounded, ending the first half.

There was not much Linardi could tell his players during the half-time break. A cross buck the Fulton team was using needed some defensing, and the defensive coach and Linardi spent some time on how to stop it. For the rest all Linardi could do was hope that the offense could get moving when they did get a chance to go again. So far, however, the Warriors had done such a fine job of controlling the ball that the outlook was not encouraging. Linardi finished the festivities with a plea to the defensive unit to do what it could to get hold of the ball by hitting just a little harder and by going for the ball on every single tackle. Gene felt it was a rather desperate plan.

Fulton received the kickoff to start the second half. But this time they ran out of steam on the

Hornet forty-two yard line and for the first time in the game, punted. Terry Lowden caught the punt on the ten and sliced his way upfield as far as the fifty before he was tripped up by the Warrior punter—the last player between the little scatback and the goal line.

Since Townsend had to play catch-up football, he put the ball in the air on the first play from scrimmage. It was a long pass to Cartwright on a fly pattern down the right sideline, an aerial bomb that could have split the game wide open. But the pass was too long for Cartwright. The end struggled valiantly to reach it, but it dropped to the turf just ahead of him. Gene slumped back down on the bench and found himself wondering if perhaps he could not have reached that pass.

After practice the day before, as Gene had started to go in with the rest of the squad, Townsend had come over and asked him to stay out for a while longer to catch some passes for him.

Gene was already bushed from the long drills he had been working on, drills designed by Linardi to help him get past linebackers and defensive backs. But he had shrugged and turned back.

"I was watching you," Townsend had remarked, as they started back to the field. "You don't look fast with that wobbly stride of yours, but you do manage to get out there. I'd like to see just what you can do."

"You pass, I'll catch," Gene said curtly.

Gene got down on his three-point stance as Townsend picked up a football and leaned over as if he were receiving the pass from center.

"Run a slant," he told Terry, then started to backpedal.

Gene took off low, cut sharply across the flat and looked back. The ball was in the air, coming hard. He increased his stride, reached out, and pulled it in.

"Okay," said Townsend, "now try a fly. Go all out. I want to see how far you can go."

Breathing heavily, Gene nodded.

He didn't look back until he had covered almost fifty yards. Then he looked up and saw the football over his head and beginning to drop. He stretched his legs and reached out. The football settled gently into his arms.

"That's the way," Townsend said curtly as Gene trotted back toward him. "Now let's try a few hooks and then we'll go for another long one."

Gene started to protest, then took a deep breath and tossed the football underhand to Townsend.

About an hour later, weary but pleased with himself, Gene trotted off the field ahead of Townsend. The quarterback had said nothing in thanks and had only nodded curtly when Gene himself had announced with finality that he was calling it a day; but there remained no doubt in Gene's mind that Townsend could pass it good and long, and that Gene could go get it. Townsend would really have to unwind if he wanted to get one beyond Gene.

Now, sitting on the bench and recalling that extended workout, Gene wished suddenly that he was in the game instead of Cartwright. He was convinced that Cartwright did not have his speed; and at the moment the long bomb was precisely what Townsend needed to get Pine Ridge back in this ball game.

A short pass over the middle to Terry Lowden kept the drive alive with a first down on the Fulton forty-five. Townsend then tried a draw up the middle with Ketchel carrying. Ketchel broke through for six yards. On the next play Townsend pitched out to Huff, who tried to skirt left end. His interference broke down, however, and he was piled under before he could turn the corner.

Third down, four yards to go.

Jim Martin nudged Gene and said, "If Townsend's got any sense, he'll give the ball to Ketchel. That draw play is working perfectly."

And that's exactly what it looked like as Townsend turned after the pass from center and appeared to hand off to Ketchel. But when he had turned back around again, Gene saw the football still in his hand. Townsend set himself and raised the football over his head. He was looking downfield.

Gene shot to his feet. Cartwright, laboring mightily, was trying to pull away from a safety man, who nevertheless was sticking to him with the persistence of a summer cold. And Hutchins was lost in a crowd of Fulton defensive backs.

Gene glanced back at Townsend. The quarterback's protection was breaking down and a lineman was circling around to come at him from his blind side. At the last possible moment, Townsend sent the ball on its flight. Cartwright struggled to move faster in an effort to catch up to the ball. His stride lengthened. He reached up. But the ball dropped just beyond his outstretched fingers.

Incomplete pass. Fourth and four.

Linardi signaled to Townsend to punt. Townsend nodded unhappily, and the huddle closed around him.

Townsend's punt put Fulton back on their own fifteen; and as Townsend trotted for the sideline, Gene saw that he was heading directly for the coach. Before he had his helmet off, he was talking with some animation to Linardi. And Linardi appeared to be listening carefully.

"Linardi should give me a chance," said Jim Martin. "Townsend's not clicking today at all. He never should have tried that last pass of his. He's just not sharp enough today."

Gene did not reply. He didn't agree with Jim. That last call had been a good one. If Cartwright had been just a little faster . . .

"Don't you think so?" Martin demanded.

Gene shrugged. "Maybe."

That response didn't satisfy Jim. He glanced with sudden annoyance at Gene, but said nothing more and turned his attention back to the field. The Hornet defense was again making like a stone wall, and for the second time in the game, Fulton was going to have to punt. The adjustment Linardi had made on the Warrior cross buck had evidently done the job. Now if only Townsend could get the offense rolling.

Lowden caught Fulton's punt on the twenty and was able to make only ten more yards before he was swarmed under.

The offensive squad poured off the bench, Townsend in the lead.

"Merrill!"

Gene looked down the bench to see Linardi waving him onto the field. An unhappy Cartwright was standing beside the coach. He was in the act of slipping out of his helmet.

"Go on out there!" Linardi cried. "And hurry it up!"

Gene made a grab for his helmet, missed, and knocked it to the ground. Furious with himself, he swept it up and raced out onto the field.

Gene didn't know if this was Linardi's idea or Townsend's, but he had a sneaking suspicion that it was the quarterback who had suggested the change—not that Gene or anyone else would ever be able to get him to admit it.

As Gene ducked into the huddle, Townsend growled: "I hope you're faster getting downfield than you are reaching a huddle."

"Try me," Gene said.

But Townsend didn't—not on the first play. He sent Ketchel up the middle, and Ketchel got five yards. Then Townsend sent Lowden around right end. On this play Gene's assignment was to take out the linebacker. After the working over Gene got on the play before that, he put his heart into the job and took the linebacker out so effectively that Lowden had no difficulty making the necessary yardage for the first down.

In the huddle Lowden grinned across at Gene. "Nice blocking, Merrill."

On the next play Townsend called Huff's number for a sweep around left end, and only a last-minute, desperation tackle prevented the big fellow from going all the way.

First down.

"Play pass," Townsend said. Then he glanced at Gene. "Fly pattern," he told Gene. To Billy Hutchins he said, "Run a short hook. I might go to you if Merrill can't get loose."

He turned then to Ketchel. "The fake'll be a delayed trap up the middle, Seth. Make it look like the real thing." The fullback nodded. "On six," Townsend told the rest of the huddle.

Gene kept his face calm as he watched the Fulton linebacker set himself across the scrimmage line. He was about five yards back. Then Gene went down onto his three-point stance, the fingers of his right hand resting lightly on the cool grass.

On six Gene plunged directly across the line of scrimmage at the linebacker, then shoulder-faked to the inside. As the linebacker made his move to the inside to block Gene out, Gene cut to the outside and swept past him. The Fulton defensive back raced over to cover; but he was not prepared for Gene's speed, and by the time he had begun to really dig in, it was too late as Gene pulled steadily ahead of him.

Gene looked back. The football was in the air, heading right toward him—or where he would be soon enough. The pass led him perfectly. He would not need to slow down at all. As he raced into the end zone, he saw—out of the corner of his eye—the Fulton deep safety racing desperately, hopelessly over to cover.

And then the ball was rushing down toward him. In full stride he reached up for it. Through his upraised arms the football plunged untouched, striking the ground just ahead of him.

Gene couldn't believe it. He felt betrayed, tricked; it was some kind of hideous joke being played on him. Then a cry of rage and disappointment burst from his lips, to be lost in the collective groan that burst from the crowd.

The Fulton safety back, still racing over, bent down, and in full stride snatched up the still tumbling football.

"This what you're looking for?" he asked, grinning.

Gene turned and started back to the huddle, a trip he dreaded. When he reached it, he glanced at Townsend.

"It was a good pass," he croaked. "I should have had it."

"That's right," Townsend said curtly. "Both times."

Townsend tried a line plunge. It netted four yards. A short pass over the middle to Hutchins gained five more. It was not enough, and Townsend was forced to punt.

"It's all my fault," Gene said a moment later from the bench as the Fulton Warriors drove to the Hornet forty-two. "When I missed that pass, it took the guts right out of us. It was a touchdown, pure and simple, and I let it go right through my arms."

"Now don't blame yourself," said Jim. "Townsend had no right putting you on the spot like that so soon. He was trying to make you look bad."

Gene looked at him in astonishment. "You must be kidding."

"No, I'm not. He hates your guts. You know that."

Gene frowned. He wanted to argue the point with his friend, but thought better of it and looked back to the field. Jim was wrong—completely wrong in his estimation of Jeff Townsend's character. But Gene saw in Jim's statement an attempt on his part to take Gene's side in this war of his with Townsend. And for that he was properly grateful.

A roar from the crowd brought both of them to their feet. Gene saw a mountain of players growing on the fifty-yard line, which meant only one thing—a loose ball!

The bodies were peeled back. A referee reached

down for the ball, then suddenly pointed in the direction of the Fulton goal. The Hornets had recovered!

Without giving Linardi a chance to consider, Gene snatched up his helmet and raced out onto the field with the rest of the offensive squad.

Townsend stayed on the ground for the first two series of downs, aware that since they were two touchdowns back, Fulton would be looking for them to pass. After two quick first downs, Fulton closed up their defense, and Townsend sent Billy Hutchins downfield on a post pattern. He hit Billy in full stride, putting the Hornets on the Warrior thirty-two.

Townsend glanced across the huddle at Huff. "Let's take it on a ride around right end, Wendell."

Huff nodded.

"On three." Townsend clapped his hands.

As Gene got ready for the snap, he went over in his mind the play Townsend had called. It was a basic sweep, in which Townsend faked a cross buck to the fullback and then pitched out to Huff coming around. Gene's job was simple. All he had to do was take out the linebacker.

And, surprisingly, it was getting to be an assignment he liked. He had been piling into the linebacker with more and more gusto as this drive continued, and he found that there was something absolutely pleasant in hurling himself at another player. It helped to ease somewhat the frustration he still felt for letting that ball go through his arms.

"Ready, set," Townsend barked. "One . . . two . . . thr . . ."

Gene launched himself across the line of scrimmage. The linebacker saw him coming, hesitated, then tried to sidestep him as he saw Huff get the pitchout and start around right end, but Gene drove into him hard and low, and the fellow stumbled backward, tripped, and fell to the ground.

Gene scrambled to his feet, his eye on another linebacker coming over fast to meet Huff. Gene kept low and flung himself into the fellow's path. The linebacker tried to swerve away, but Gene caught him perfectly, right below the knees, and the fellow went down. As Gene lifted his face out of the grass and looked up, he saw Huff pound past him and head down the sideline.

Still on his hands and knees, Gene saw Huff get hit on the five-yard line, spin off the tackler, stumble once, twice, then fall forward over the goal line, a Fulton tackler still clinging to his back.

Touchdown!

A moment later Townsend sent the ball cartwheeling between the uprights to make it seven to thirteen.

As Gene trotted off the field, Wendell pulled

up beside him. "That's real blocking there, Gene. You really took those guys out nicely. Looks like you enjoy your work."

"Thanks, Wendell. I guess I do. I didn't think I would, but I do. Now if I could only catch the ball."

"Don't worry about that, Gene. I don't think Townsend is."

But Jim Martin had other ideas, a complete reversal of what he had felt earlier, when he had stated that Townsend was deliberately throwing to Gene to put him on the spot.

"He's deliberately freezing you out, Gene," Jim said. "And that's not fair. You got down there fast that last time, and you did a nice job of fooling the safety. You should be given another chance."

"Oh, it's all right, Jim," Gene replied mildly. "We got on the scoreboard finally, and that's what counts."

"Maybe. But we haven't won it yet—and it doesn't look like we're going to, either."

Gene frowned and looked out at the field. It was true. Things did not look good. There were only eight minutes left and the Fulton quarterback was playing his usual time-consuming game, staying on the ground and being content to grind out his first downs with three and four yard gains. And this time he seemed to have found the combination that had worked so well in the first half.

"Hold! Hold!" Gene muttered minutes later as he watched the Hornet defensive line dig in desperately. They had been pushed back to their thirty-yard line with only three minutes left on the clock.

The Fulton quarterback took the snap and handed off to his halfback. The fellow skirted the left end without too much trouble, but before he could get rolling downfield, a hurtling Hornet linebacker hit him high at the same moment that another tackler hit him low. The ball carrier flipped up, then over—and as he did, the ball popped out of his arms and shot high into the air. Gene heard himself shouting wildly as first one player and then another batted at the ball.

And then it hit the ground. Instantly a rapidly growing mound of frantically grabbing players grew over the ball. Whistle screeching, the referee started pulling off the players. At last he dug out the ball and made his signal.

Again it was Pine Ridge's ball!

Gene grabbed his helmet.

A fullback slant over right tackle got nowhere, so the left guard glared across the huddle at Townsend and insisted that the next play go over him. Townsend nodded. Huff got the call and crashed over left guard for five yards. Third and five.

Townsend glanced at Gene. "Slant in, Merrill. This'll be a quick one." He looked around the huddle. "On four."

Gene trotted over to his spot and ducked down, no reflection of his pounding heart visible on his calm face. Townsend moved quickly up over the center. On four both lines sprang to life, and Gene darted straight for the linebacker.

Wary now, the linebacker hesitated. At once Gene cut inside and spurted past him. The back lunged at Gene, but missed completely.

Gene turned. The football was in the air, leading him perfectly. He grabbed it. As he tucked it away, he was hit from the left side, then the back. Twisting and turning, he kept moving forward until a crushing blow from the right brought him down.

They had to bring in the chain to measure it, but the gain was good for a first down with less than two minutes left to play.

A trap play up the middle netted Ketchel twelve more yards and put the Hornets in Warrior territory, but the clock was still running. Townsend threw a sideline pass to Billy Hutchins, who caught the ball six yards further downfield and immediately stepped out of bounds to stop the clock.

One minute left.

"Merrill," Townsend said, "let's try that same play pass we tried before. And Merrill—this time, catch it."

Gene nodded.

The linebacker gave Gene a good shove, but Gene managed to stay on his feet, straighten up, and take off down the sideline. He kept just a little speed in reserve until the deep safety closed with him. Then as soon as Gene saw that the back was matching him stride for stride, he increased his speed and spurted past him.

He looked back. Townsend was just getting the ball off. But it was a desperation heave, and Gene could tell that the ball would come down in the end zone at such a steep angle that it just might be anyone's ball.

His eyes on the football, Gene crossed into the end zone. At the same time he was aware of footsteps other than his own pounding closer and closer. Suddenly a Fulton back reached up to catch the ball, his arm partly obscuring Gene's view of the football. Gene turned around and leaped high, thrusting his body between the ball and the Fulton player. The ball thumped heavily against his chest.

He grappled it to him. At almost the same instant another back hit him from behind. Gene felt the air whoosh out of his lungs. He was flung violently forward to the ground—the ball still hugged tightly to his chest. Above the sustained roar of the crowd, he heard the welcome shriek of the referee's whistle and knew that it was a touchdown this time.

As he got slowly to his feet and handed the ball to the referee, he found himself wondering if Townsend would succeed in kicking the extra point—the point they still needed to win this game.

Townsend did.

When Gene stepped into the parking lot in back of the locker room after his hot shower, he felt only the glow of triumph. The memory of that muffed pass had been replaced by another, better one; and the aches and pains wouldn't come until later. At the moment it felt good just to be alive. He looked around.

Some students were still hanging around the lot, and Gene caught sight of Ronny Kline standing by a sleek white convertible talking to the girl behind the wheel. The girl was Barbara Collins.

Gene decided that this was one day he could throw caution to the wind and let bygones be bygones.

"Hi, Ronny," he called as he neared them. "Hi, Barbara!"

Barbara just nodded to him.

"Nice game," said Ronny. "A real thriller."

Gene nodded to Ronny, then glanced down at Barbara. "New car?"

"The family lets me take it out on special occasions."

"What's so special today?"

"There's a dance at the country club."

"Country club, huh?" He looked at Ronny.

"Not me!" Ronny said, laughing. "Don't look at me!"

A hard finger tapped Gene on his shoulder. He spun around and found himself looking into Jeff Townsend's handsome face. The quarterback was dressed in a white sports jacket with a thin string tie. His shirt was white and his slacks were a dark maroon. He had shaved, and there was a careless-looking, but most artfully arranged, curl in his hair. He looked as if he had just stepped out of a men's fashion magazine, not off a football field.

Gene stepped aside without a word as Townsend moved past Gene and got into the car. With a careless wave, Barbara drove off.

Gene stood beside Ronny and watched them disappear. He tried to tell himself it was good riddance, but he couldn't.

"What's up?" said Ronny. "I thought you had the inside track with Barbara."

Gene shook his head. "I'm not country club material."

"Neither is Barbara, Gene."

"Well, that's where she's going with Golden Boy."

"Well, anyway, you've got to feel pretty good. I mean after a game like that, how can you kick? After all, you can't have everything."

Gene smiled bleakly at Ronny. His friend was obviously just trying to cheer him up. But the trouble was you *could* have everything—if you were Jeff Townsend and you were sitting beside Barbara Collins in a white convertible.

8

GENE HURRIED DOWN the stairs and pulled open the door. Ronny Kline was standing in the doorway, dressed in a dark blue sports coat, white shirt, and tie. His slacks were neatly pressed, and even his shoes were polished. A bright green sedan was parked at the curb, and Gene saw a vaguely familiar, dark-haired girl sitting in the front seat.

"Hey," Ronny said, "aren't you going?"

"The Halloween Dance?"

"Sure!"

Gene shrugged.

"Come on! Don't be an old stick-in-the-mud! Throw something on. Fran and I'll wait in the car." He grinned suddenly. "And don't worry. It won't be lonesome."

Surprised and pleased that Ronny had thought of him at all, Gene made up his mind quickly. "Sure!" he said. "Be right down. Won't take me a minute."

As he closed the door, he saw his mother in the living room doorway. "Going somewhere, Gene?"

"The Halloween Dance!" he called as he bolted up the stairs to his room.

Gene paused in the gym doorway. The place was decorated with long streamers of orangc and black crepe paper, hanging in great loops from the ceiling, and paper pumpkins and black cats Scotch-taped to the walls. A fierce, piercing, amplified sound rent the air, while all over the polished gym floor couples casually gyrated and wriggled in front of each other—a look of soulful pain on their faces.

The frantic sound was coming from a slightly raised platform at the far end of the gym, where a local group called The Beards had set themselves up. The group consisted of a drummer, two electric guitarists, and a vocalist who stomped his feet a lot and held a death grip on the microphone.

Wincing from the sound, Gene stepped into the gym with Ronny and Fran.

"Well now, how do you like The Beards?" Ronny half shouted.

"They're so loud, I can't hear them," Gene shouted back.

Fran laughed at Gene's reply, but her laughter was at once swept up in the torrent of amplified sound, like a straw in a hurricane. Grinning and waving goodbye to Gene, Ronny pulled Fran out onto the gym floor.

Gene watched them for a moment, then realized how strange he must look standing there alone in the entrance to the gym. He looked quickly around to find any others that might be in the same boat as himself and saw the gym wall lined with disdainful males, who had obviously only come to the dance to stand and smirk at the twisting couples on the dance floor. Gene walked over to the wall. A fellow he vaguely recognized moved to one side to give him a clear portion of the wall for himself.

Gene stood for a long while, watching, trying to get used to the sound level of the music. Then abruptly it stopped, and the couples broke to form a heavy throng around the fringes of the dance floor. Ronny and Fran found Gene and pushed through the crush toward him.

"Hey, don't be a wallflower, Gene," Ronny protested. "You're Big Man on Campus—a member of the football team. Make yourself known to these girls."

"I don't dance very well."

Ronny turned to Fran. "Did you hear that? The fastest man on the team, and he says he doesn't dance. What can you do about that?"

Fran grinned, her large dark eyes glowing. With a quick movement of her right hand she brushed her long curls back over her shoulder. "You come out onto the floor with me," she insisted. "Next dance I'll show you how. It's easy, honest."

"Well . . ."

The Beards started up again, louder and even more frenzied than before.

Fran shouted up at him, "Come on!"

Grabbing his hand, she pulled him out onto the gym floor, faced him, and began to twist. Watching carefully, Gene tried to follow her lead: when she bent forward and backward, he did so as well and, as best he could, matched her wriggle for wriggle, twist for twist. But he could not get himself to feel comfortable doing so. And he kept bumping into other couples around him. After a while he found himself wishing that the music would stop and he could retreat back to that comforting wall.

At last the music stopped.

"Thanks a lot, Fran," he said, taking her hand and pulling her quickly toward the sidelines.

So anxious was he to get off the dance floor, however, that he collided sharply with a couple moving in the other direction. He looked down in surprise, anxious to apologize—and found himself face to face with Barbara Collins and Jeff Townsend. The apology froze on his lips. He tried to say something, but the sudden ache in the pit of his stomach would not let the words come. Confused and suddenly miserable, he pushed past Barbara and continued off the dance floor.

"Hold it just a minute there," said Jeff, as

he grabbed Gene's arm and spun him around. "Who do you think you're shoving, anyway?"

Those dancers around them immediately froze. A fight! Gene could see the quick eagerness in their eyes as they moved closer to get a better view of the action. Swiftly they enclosed Gene and Townsend in a ring of intent faces.

Gene felt Fran's hand freeing itself from his as she melted into the crowd. The Beards started up again, but the sound seemed to have receded as the throbbing of his own pulse filled his ears. Townsend pushed still closer to him, his cold, angry eyes boring into Gene's.

"I said who do you think you're shoving anyway?" Townsend repeated, his voice low, menacing.

"I—I didn't mean to push her," Gene said.

"Well, you *did* push her," Townsend insisted, moving still closer. "You pushed her aside like she was some kind of peasant that got in your way. And I think you bumped into us deliberately."

"No, I did not bump into you deliberately," Gene insisted, aware that his voice shook as he spoke. "But if you want to make something of it, come right ahead."

"Sure, I want to make something of it. You can't go around knocking people like . . ."

"Jeff!" Barbara pleaded, pulling at Townsend.

"Please! Gene didn't mean it. Leave him alone!"

He looked down at her, then back at Gene. For the first time he seemed aware of the hushed, expectant ring of faces. He pulled himself erect and took a half step back. "All right," he said. "But this guy better watch where he's going in the future. And he still hasn't apologized."

"Never *mind,*" she insisted angrily. "I want you to stop this foolishness right now. Either that or take me home!"

Gene looked at Barbara. "I *am* sorry I bumped into you, Barbara, and I didn't mean to push you aside like that. Honest. Are you all right?"

She looked at him and tried to smile. "Yes, Gene," she said, her face coloring. "I'm fine."

Then she pulled on Townsend's arm. He went with her without protest, and the crowd around them broke up. Gene moved back to the wall.

But now the noise from The Beards seemed suddenly *too* loud, more than he could stand; he felt almost sick to his stomach. Cold sweat stood out on his forehead. Pushing himself away from the wall, he turned and headed for the gym door. For a moment he hesitated and looked back at the seething dance floor. He wanted to say goodbye to Ronny and Fran and to thank them. But he couldn't see them in the crush of dancers.

The music climbed a few more decibels, and he turned and hurried out.

Once outside in the cold October night, he took a deep breath and felt immediately better. But he did not want to go home, not yet.

He had begun to sense how pleased his parents were at his success on the football field and at the fact that he was no longer content to keep to himself. As soon as Gene had noticed this, he realized how troubled they must have been at his earlier withdrawn behavior—behavior which they, surprisingly, had appeared to encourage. Coming home now, long before the dance was over, would reveal to them just how pathetic was this effort of his to join in and to become a part of the life of this town.

A short burst of laughter behind him, uttered by a couple leaving the gym together, caused him to start up suddenly and head off across the parking lot. When he reached the sidewalk, he started swiftly down the tree-darkened street, his hands thrust deep into his pockets, his head down, his face averted from those few he passed. A scalding bitterness was welling up within him at the thought of how eagerly Townsend had turned on him. He had hoped that some kind of understanding might have developed between them during these past three games, but now it was obvious that nothing had changed between them. It was the same old Townsend, eager to hurt him in any way that he could.

And this was the kind of guy Barbara preferred. For the hundredth time, he tried to tell himself that he no longer cared about Barbara Collins—that she was not for him. She deserved Townsend and Townsend deserved her.

"Gene! Hey, Gene!"

Gene pulled up sharply and turned. It was Bill Wittington standing on the corner across the street with a large bag of groceries in his hand.

"Oh, hello, Bill. How's it going?"

"Skip's home, Gene. He got in a little while ago." Bill indicated the bag of groceries with a nod of his head. "We're celebrating!"

"That's fine, Billy. Guess I'll stop around and say hello."

"Sure! Come ahead. He's dying to hear how you're doing on the team."

Gene waved and continued on.

When he came to his own street, however, he hurried past it and walked on until he had reached the town's outer limits. At last, when he came to the railroad crossing, he followed the tracks back to town and cut up Orchard Street to his house.

A light was on in the kitchen and in his father's room. He mounted the porch step carefully and let himself in the front door without a sound. Then, just as silently, he moved up the stairs and into his room. Taking off his shoes very carefully, he lay back cautiously on his bed and remained in that position, staring up at the ceiling and listening to the beating of his heart. From the television set below him in the living room came snatches of dialogue and the sound of canned laughter. But he did not hear either his mother or his father joining in the laughter. As usual, they were probably not watching it.

The doorbell rang. Gene closed his eyes. He had expected it. Holding his breath, he listened as his mother's heavy steps travelled the length of the kitchen, through the living room, and into the hallway. He heard her open the door. There was a surprised greeting, and then Gene recognized the deep, hearty rumble of Skip's voice. Straining his ears, Gene heard his mother tell Skip that Gene was at the Halloween Dance.

Then Gene heard Skip explaining to his mother that his kid brother had seen Gene walking up Market Street about an hour ago and had assumed from this that Gene had left the dance and was on his way home. There was a moment's discussion, after which Gene heard his mother go to the foot of the stairs.

"Gene!" she called. "You up there?"

Gene opened his mouth. The words were waiting, ready and eager to tumble out. Yes! He was up here, lying in the dark, waiting for a friend to come by! He'd be right down!

"Gene! Are you up there?"

Gene closed his eyes and clenched his fists. There was a pause, and then Gene's mother said something to Skip. Skip's hearty laughter sounded out for a moment, after which the screen door slammed. Gene heard his mother close the inside door and then her footsteps as she returned to the kitchen. On her way through the living room, she turned off the television set.

Slowly Gene undressed in the darkness. The next morning he would tell his mother that he had come in long after they were all asleep, and that he had come in as silently as possible so as not to awaken them. If his mother mentioned Skip's visit, he would express his disappointment at having missed his friend.

Gene climbed into bed and pulled the covers up around him. Barbara did not deserve Townsend, not really. In fact, that very evening in the midst of all that unpleasantness, she had revealed an almost protective concern for Gene—and along with it a spark of impatience and even anger at Townsend for his belligerent behavior. Gene recalled this with sudden vividness as hope sprang alive within him.

But Barbara did not approve of Gene's friendship with Skip, and if she were to see him this weekend with the tall Negro, that would be the end for him; Townsend would have a clear field.

Gene rolled over in the darkness and pulled the covers up over his shoulders. He felt suddenly cold—and utterly and completely ashamed of himself. He knew now that he would continue to avoid Skip for the rest of the weekend.

9

A PLAY HAD just been busted, and Townsend had had to eat the ball. As Gene turned wearily about and trotted back, he saw that Townsend was slow in getting up. Gene was not surprised. Half the Spartan team had caught Townsend back there.

That was the kind of game it had been so far. They were halfway through the third quarter and still had not been able to score. Though the Hannibal Spartans had scored a touchdown early in the first quarter, they had been unable to score again. It had been a brutal defensive slugging match ever since, with Gene painfully aware that much of Pine Ridge's difficulty could be traced directly back to his own erratic performance. Two passes already in the game he had dropped, the last one toward the end of the first half. Had he hung on to it, it would have been good for a long gain. Gene could still recall how the exultant roar from the crowd collapsed into a massive groan when the ball bounced away from him.

Closer now to Townsend, Gene watched as the quarterback shook his head blearily and tried to get to his feet. It looked like Townsend was in trouble as he finally got to his feet and started for the huddle. Before he could reach it, Jim Martin raced onto the field and told him to take a rest. Without protest, Townsend turned and trotted slowly off the field.

As Gene reached the huddle, Jim glanced at him. "Okay, Gene," he said, clapping his hands together. "*Now* we go all the way!"

Gene was a little surprised at the implications of the remark, as were the other players. Did Jim feel that Townsend was well out of the game—that now with him, Jim Martin, at the controls, they would finally be able to get rolling? If so, it revealed an astonishing lack of awareness on Jim's part. Not only was Townsend a superlative quarterback; each player on the team—and that included Gene—knew it.

It was funny. Though Gene hated Townsend and had no doubt in his mind that Townsend hated him just as thoroughly, he had no difficulty at all in acknowledging what a fine quarterback he was.

"We're going to try that cross-over, Gene," Jim said. "I've been watching from the bench. You can beat that defensive back covering you, and the deep safety is too lazy to come in where he should. You ought to be wide open."

Gene nodded.

Jim quickly went over the other assignments, gave the snap signal, and clapped his hands. If decisiveness and a clear picture of the job ahead were assets a quarterback needed, Jim appeared to have them in abundance. Gene was glad that his friend was going to have this chance to prove himself.

The huddle broke smartly, and the players moved up to the line looking very much alive. It was second and fourteen. If this pass play clicked they'd get the fourteen yards and then some. If not, Jim's options would narrow considerably.

On the snap Gene broke across the line of scrimmage, darted past the linebacker, who made only a half-hearted attempt to stop him, then moved swiftly downfield. As the Hannibal back raced over to cover him, Gene executed a quick shoulder-fake outside, then broke past him on the inside. Before the fellow could recover, Gene had pulled well ahead of him. And just as Jim had said he would, the deep safety began to back-pedal instead of moving in to cover.

Gene looked back. The football was already in the air, but off target—behind Gene and to his right. Gene pulled up quickly, turned, and dived for the football. He had possession of the ball for only an instant—until he hit the ground. The impact broke his grip, and the ball bounced away.

The referee, whistle screeching, raced over, his arms waving frantically. Incomplete pass.

Gene took a deep breath and got unhappily to his feet. He had been in the clear. If the pass had been long enough and on target, maybe—just maybe—he might have gone all the way.

Gene was almost to the huddle when he noticed Jim pacing unhappily a couple of yards back from the other players. At the same time he caught a few glances from the other players, who seemed to be looking at him with some apprehension, as if they expected some kind of a blow up. Gene slowed. What was wrong?

The huddle formed. Jim stopped pacing and moved into it, his face grim.

"Too bad," Gene said. "I could have gone all the way if that ball had been thrown just a trifle more accurately. Like you said he would, Jim, that safety . . ."

"You saying that was a bad pass?" demanded Jim, breaking in.

Gene was astonished at Jim's tone. "Well, what did it look like to you?"

"I'll tell you what it looked like to me, Gimpy! You didn't run that pattern the way you should have! With that wobbly stride of yours, you were all over the field. You looked like a wagon with one wheel off!"

Gene realized how important it was for Jim that he supplant Jeff Townsend as the team's number one quarterback. It was this that drove him to second-guess Townsend constantly. All this Gene knew perfectly. For this reason he understood why Jim was so dismayed that his pass to Gene had not clicked. But it made no difference. Gene was stunned—and then angrier than he had ever been before in his life.

"Well, thanks, Jim," Gene said tightly. "I'll keep that criticism in mind the next time I go out."

Then he ducked his head and waited for Jim to call the next play. He heard Jim clear his throat nervously and call for a routine line plunge up the middle, Ketchel carrying.

Only dimly was Gene aware of himself leaving the huddle and shifting into his three-point stance; and when the snap came, it was as if a spring had been released within him. He hurtled across the line of scrimmage at the hapless Hannibal linebacker and caught him just below the midsection. As the fellow buckled forward, Gene lifted his shoulder and caught him squarely in the chest, then flung him back. There was a surprised grunt followed by the sharp clunk the back's shoulder pads and helmet made as they slammed the turf.

Gene kept on, looking for someone else to flatten. Before he could find anyone, however, the play was blown dead. Though Ketchel had gained six yards on the play, it was not nearly enough for the first down, which meant they would have to punt.

Gene turned and looked toward the bench. Townsend was hurrying onto the field to make the punt. Cooling down somewhat and pleased to see that Townsend was all right, Gene went back and helped the still groggy linebacker to his feet.

After all, he thought sourly as he headed back to the huddle, that Spartan back wasn't Jim Martin—only a handy substitute.

While the Pine Ridge defense tried to contain the Hannibal offense, Gene sat numbly on an isolated corner of the bench and tried to get his thoughts into some kind of order. He needed to know why Jim Martin had kept his animosity hidden from Gene this long—and why it had taken Gene so long to realize what kind of a guy . . .

"Come on, Gene! Let's go!"

Gene looked down the bench and saw the offensive team spilling back onto the field, Townsend in the lead. Glancing out at the playing field, Gene saw a Pine Ridge player pushing himself off the ground and handing to the referee the loose football he had just covered with his body.

"Hit them when they're depressed," Townsend told the huddle. "So now's the time for the long bomb." He looked across the huddle at Gene. "Remember that fly pattern you ran in the Fulton game? I've been saving that one. So let's try it again, but this time put some glue on those hands of yours."

Wincing, Gene nodded.

A moment later as the huddle broke and Gene trotted over to his position, he felt little if any nervousness. He was just anxious to get going down that sideline, grimly determined to prove to Jim Martin watching from the bench that, gimpy leg or not, he could hang on to the ball as long as it was thrown correctly.

On the snap he lunged across the line of scrimmage and headed directly for the linebacker. The fellow braced himself; as soon as he did so, Gene cut past him to the outside and headed down the sideline. He did not run flat out until the defensive back hurrying over to cover was within a few feet of him. Abruptly, Gene shifted into high and shot past him. Only then did he really turn it on as he fairly flew down the sideline.

He glanced back. The football was already in the air, and *this* time it was not underthrown. If anything, it was perhaps too long. Gene dug harder as the football began to drop. He increased the length of his stride and then—timing his leap perfectly—launched himself high into the air. His right hand caught the nose of the football and slammed it back against his chest.

He came down with both arms wrapped securely around the football. He was less than five yards from the end zone and lunged for it. A Spartan tackler struck him just below his left hip, then went spinning off. The impact, however, was enough to turn Gene completely around. Another tackler crashed into him then, but Gene twisted away, managed to spin around and dive a second time for the goal line. But a third tackler hit him from the side and cut him down less than two yards from the end zone.

As Gene neared the huddle moments later, the players acknowledged his fine catch with broad smiles. A few clapped him on the back. Even Ketchel seemed pleased.

But Townsend was scowling. "Okay, okay," he said. "But what took you so long getting downfield?"

Feeling much too good to argue, Gene just shrugged and ducked into the huddle. "Beats me," he said.

Townsend snorted and gave the next play: a swift opener up the middle with Ketchel carrying.

It was funny, Gene noted, as he moved up to the line of scrimmage a moment later. Townsend refused to join in with the rest of the team's enthusiasm for Gene's catch; yet it didn't bother Gene a bit. He had kind of expected it. In fact, he had even looked forward to it.

Ketchel carried a foolhardy linebacker into the end zone with him for the touchdown, and a moment later Townsend's kick for the extra point was good, tying the score at seven all.

Not long after, the fired-up Hornet defense got the ball back a second time—on this occasion by intercepting a pass—and in the closing minutes of the final quarter, Townsend sent Huff on a wide sweep around right end. After taking out the linebacker with as nice a block as he had thrown all afternoon, Gene looked up to see the bottom of Huff's cleats hurdling both Gene and the linebacker. Huff got to the five-yard line before he was knocked out of bounds, leaving Townsend with all of a minute to get the ball into the end zone.

Townsend called another sweep around the right end, then tucked the football on his left hip and loped, unscathed, into the end zone.

Forty seconds later the game was over with the final score: Pine Ridge fourteen, Hannibal seven.

The memory of the team's victory did not entirely fade for Gene until he dropped at last onto his bed later that day. The excitement had prevented him from eating a very large supper—the excitement and the weariness. He was, as usual, sore all over.

He lay on his back on the bed and closed his eyes and took a deep breath.

And then in a rush he was back out on that field looking across the huddle in stunned disbelief as Jim's cruel words sank in, words that were still digging at him—like fish hooks. He sat up.

Jim Martin and Jeff Townsend certainly had a right to be upset with his erratic play thus far this season. And perhaps Gene should have hung on to Jim's pass. His performance up to that moment in the game had not been one calculated to inspire confidence. But did that warrant Jim's vicious outburst, his calling Gene Gimpy with such obvious relish? Others, of course, had used that term as well, and Gene was used to it by now; but coming from Jim Martin—the only player on the team he had come to regard as his friend—it was almost too much to bear.

He knew now that Jim Martin was *not* his friend and never had been. All this time Jim had been hiding from Gene his true feelings, his honest revulsion at Gene's limp and at the crooked way he seemed to run.

How much kinder it would have been for Jim to have spoken and acted toward him with the same blunt honesty displayed by Townsend and

Ketchel. Their feelings were out in the open—not hidden, like something scurrying out from under a rock. Perhaps they did hate Gene's guts, but at least they made no secret of it. Gene could deal with that.

A disquieting thought occurred to Gene. If he was accusing Jim of not being honest with him, didn't that same accusation apply to himself? Just how honest had *he* been with Skip Wittington?

Gene left his bed and walked to his window and looked out. For the first time in almost three weeks, he allowed himself to examine coldly just what he had done Halloween weekend. It had not been easy avoiding Skip. Two more times Skip had called at his house and each time Gene had not been home for him. Once on Market Street he'd seen Skip coming and had ducked into a store. It had not been a very pretty performance. Involuntarily, Gene shuddered. He was looking into a mirror and seeing only ugliness.

Gene turned away from the window and walked over to his small desk in the corner and sat down. He thought a moment, then reached for some paper. He owed Skip a letter—a long one and an honest one.

10

As Gene's father turned off the clover leaf and started down Hamilton's main street toward the stadium, Gene turned around in the front seat and smiled at his mother. She was sitting between Emma and Fred Wittington. Billy had not come. He was on the freshman football team and had a game that Saturday.

"Think you might do it, huh, Mom?" said Gene.

Fred Wittington grinned back at Gene. "I think she's weakening, Gene."

"Those marvelous stoves," Mrs. Wittington said, shaking her head. "I don't blame her."

"Well, Mom?" Gene prompted.

"I'll still have to think about it," she said firmly. She looked at Fred then. "But your offer *is* tempting, I must admit. It's just hard to believe that those modern stoves can do all you say they can. I don't know if I really should trust them with one of my cakes or pies. Doughnuts I'm not so worried about—but pies and cakes." She shook her head. "I don't know."

"The only real difference in cooking," said Fred, "is the length of time it takes for each item to be baked. The ingredients are still the same—and that's what make a Ma Merrill cake."

"I wonder," said Gene's mother. "I wonder if it's as simple as that. Perhaps what makes a Ma Merrill cake is the length of time it takes to bake."

Gene turned back around as his father made a turn onto a tree-lined street. On the corner there had been a large sign that read STADIUM PARKING; and sure enough, at the far end of the street a huge parking lot opened before them. And beyond it the walls of the stadium stood higher than the trees.

As they drove into the parking lot, Gene noticed four white panel trucks with NBC GAME OF THE WEEK printed in large red letters on their sides. A dark river of cable spilled out from the open backs of the trucks and poured toward the stadium.

Skip had been right. This game was going to be nationally televised.

A white-capped policeman beckoned them still further into the parking lot, and a few minutes later they pulled to a stop inches from the stadium wall.

It had been a long ride; and as soon as Gene emerged from the car, he took advantage of the opportunity to indulge himself in a nice, long, luxurious stretch. Then he hastened to help his mother and Emma Wittington out of the car.

"Skip said he'd be waiting for us at Gate H," said Mr. Wittington as he carefully put his hat back on and looked around. "And remember. He's got the tickets."

"That boy just doesn't trust the mails," Mrs. Wittington said, shaking her head.

"Do you blame him?" asked Gene's father.

Fred chuckled. "No. I guess not."

Gene smiled. According to Skip's mother, Skip had so much trouble getting the tickets that when he did finally get them, he didn't want to trust them to the mails and decided to deliver them in person at the stadium before the game. Gene was not exactly looking forward to the meeting, however, since as yet he had received no reply to his letter.

"Over there," said Gene's father, pointing to the third entrance down from where they were. Gene looked and saw, just above it, a large, fading yellow H.

"That's it," said Fred. "Looks like we won't have far to go."

But it took much longer than they expected since they had to skirt the almost solid ranks of parked cars before they reached the gate. At last they caught sight of Skip. He was standing to the right of the entrance, leaning back against the ivy-covered wall of the stadium. His mother called out to him. Skip saw them and pushed himself away from the wall. He hurried toward them, and the warmth of his smile melted most of Gene's uneasiness.

"Thought you might have got caught in the traffic!" Skip called before he reached them.

And then he flung his arms around his mother in a quick, affectionate hug, after which he shook hands with his father, who grinned proudly up into his son's face. Gene could not help noticing how much Skip had filled out since that past summer, and he was sporting a rather handsome mustache.

"Going to win?" Mr. Merrill asked, shaking Skip's hand.

"You bet we are—no matter what those sports writers say."

Then Skip greeted Gene's mother, and turned and looked squarely at Gene.

"Hi, Gene. Good to see you!"

Then he looked back at his folks. "I haven't much time. I have to be dressed in less than a half hour, so here's the tickets."

They crowded closer then; and as Skip gave out the tickets, he explained where he thought the seats might be. Though he had tried to get them all on the fifty-yard line, he had not been entirely successful. Still, they were high and were close to the fifty, which assured them of a fine view of the action.

Before they left to search for their seats, Skip pulled Gene to one side.

"Gene, Jeff Townsend's going to meet me after the game so I can introduce him to the coach. I told him to meet me here. If you see him wandering around looking for this gate, take him in tow, will you?"

"Sure, Skip."

"Okay, Gene. See you after the game."

Gene nodded and watched Skip hurry off. He seemed okay—and yet, was Gene imagining it, or did he detect a bit of make-believe in Skip's attitude toward him? Now Gene knew what it was like not to know where one stood with a friend.

The first half was all State—and Skip Wittington. Lightning struck in the very first series of downs when Skip arched a long pass half the length of the field to an end who just managed to stagger under it. Three plays later, the Hawks had scored.

In the second quarter, mixing his running plays and his short passes with devastating effect, Skip drove his team the length of the field for another touchdown; thus confounding the experts, who had predicted that the Bengals from Alfred Tech would not allow the Hawks to score more than a single touchdown.

But the game was not yet over.

On the opening kick-off of the second half, the Bengal fullback—a nationwide star on everyone's All-American—caught the ball on his ten-yard line, broke through a crowd of orange-and-gold jerseys, and took off down the right sideline. Only a last minute, desperation tackle on the State's fifteen prevented him from going all the way.

A short pass into the left flat gained twelve yards for the Bengals. Then the same fullback tore through the left side of the State line and bulled his way into the end zone.

A moment later it was fourteen to seven, and the Alfred Tech fans were whooping it up.

And they kept right on whooping it up when, later in the third quarter, a short, safety-valve pass to that same fullback turned into a spectacular run that ended on the ten-yard line. A moment later it was all tied up—fourteen to fourteen.

The final quarter was a rugged, bone-bruising ordeal for both teams as they slugged it out for meager gains that decided nothing and led to three punts and a futile field goal attempt. Finally, with less than five minutes showing on the scoreboard, Skip got his offense moving again. He seemed to have found a weakness on the left side of the line and began to exploit it. This, coupled with short passes into the flat to both his ends and his slot back, accounted for three quick first downs as the Hawks moved steadily upfield.

Then, when they reached the Bengal forty, two line plunges in a row failed to gain a yard. On third and nine Skip went back to pass—a call everyone in the stadium expected. Predictably, the Bengal's had their blitz on full; it demolished Skip's protection and sent him racing out of his pocket. He tried to get the pass off while still on the run, but was caught from behind.

That made it fourth and sixteen. Though State was on the Bengal forty-five, the coach started to send in the kicking team. But Skip waved them back, and the crowd roared its approval.

The huddle that followed was a long one. Gene looked at the clock. It had been stopped for a time out with only a minute and twenty-five seconds showing. The huddle broke.

Gene knew that Skip would pass—that he would have to pass.

Nevertheless, instead of darting back into his pocket after the snap, Skip spun to his right and handed off to his left halfback coming around. The guards had pulled out and were leading the way around the right side of the line with bruising effectiveness. Abruptly, the back pulled up, whirled, and passed the ball back to Skip standing all alone behind the line of scrimmage. The crowd gasped as Skip reached up and casually plucked the wobbly pass out of the air.

Gene looked downfield and saw the left end less than ten yards from the end zone—and completely alone. Striding carefully, Skip lofted the ball to him. The end increased his stride just enough, swept in under the ball, and hugged it to him with a care and a determination that Gene appreciated fully. A moment later he raced—untouched—over the goal line as the crowd went wild.

The kick for the point after was good—but definitely anti-climactic; and though the Bengals managed to complete a pass after they got the ball back in the closing seconds of the game, no one was really paying much attention.

When the gun sounded, State was still ahead by seven points, and the football field was a seething mass of frenzied students and fans who had swept down out of the stands with seemingly only one end in view—to grab hold of Skip or any other available member of the victorious team.

With a shout Gene left his parents and hurried down to the field. But once there, he found it impossible to manage any kind of sensible navigation in the swirling crowd of students. At last he abandoned any hope of seeing Skip or of getting to the goal posts, and hurried back up into the seats and started for the gate where he was supposed to meet Skip.

He got to Gate H before his parents, but not—he noticed—before Jeff Townsend. Townsend was standing just to one side of the entrance.

Gene stopped. Was that Barbara with him? Yes, it was. Who else would Townsend take with him to this game? Gene compressed his lips grimly and started up again.

Barbara looked uncommonly pretty as she stood beside Townsend, her cheeks rosy from the cold, a portion of her blond hair peeking out from under the white pile lining of her hood. She was wearing black slacks, brown leather boots, and a blue corduroy car coat. She looked pretty, he told himself for the second time—too pretty. He wondered miserably if he was ever going to stop pestering himself about Barbara Collins.

"Waiting for Skip?" Gene asked as he approached. He kept both hands in his pockets and did not look at Barbara.

"That's right," said Townsend. "He told me to meet him here."

Gene nodded. "Well, he'll probably be late getting out of that dressing room. He'll probably have to be interviewed by a lot of reporters, I imagine."

"That's okay," Townsend replied. "I can wait."

Gene found that he could avoid looking directly at Barbara no longer. "Hi, Barbara."

"Hi, Gene," she said.

He thought he might have detected a slight tremor in her voice, but she looked quickly away from him and turned to Townsend. "How long do you think we'll have to wait?"

Townsend shrugged.

That didn't seem to satisfy her. She sighed and looked back at Gene. "It was quite a game, Gene, wasn't it."

"Yes, it was," he said stiffly.

At that moment Gene's mother and father came into view, pushing their way through the crush that was pouring out through the gate. And right behind them came Skip's parents.

Gene's mother and father were smiling, but the broad grins on the face of Skip's folks would have melted an Alaskan glacier. To say they were happy and proud was only to scratch the surface.

"He told me about that last play," said Skip's father as he neared Gene. "He said he hoped he never had to use it in a game. Said it was too wild! He said it was not his style!" He shook his head. "Not his style!"

Gene laughed along with him and then introduced Barbara and Townsend to his and to Skip's parents, after which everyone shook hands and stood around discussing the game.

That kept them busy for some time, but at length Gene's father glanced at his watch and said, "We'll have to get moving soon if we want to get back by supper."

"Get back by supper!" Fred Wittington exclaimed. "We are all having dinner here in Hamilton. I've already made the reservations—and our two young guests are welcome to join us."

"Thank you, Mr. Wittington," Jeff said, "but I'm supposed to meet . . ." He stopped then and pointed.

They turned to see Skip striding quickly toward them with a small, stocky man by his side. The fellow's face was ruddy, and he had keen, piercing eyes and a shock of white hair brushed straight back.

"It's Coach Ward," said Skip's father.

"Sorry I'm late," Skip said when he reached them. "But those reporters wouldn't let me go." He shook his head. "And they sure ask the craziest questions."

"And the same questions," added Coach Ward, "over and over."

Skip then introduced the coach to Gene and to Gene's parents and then to Barbara and Jeff Townsend.

"So this is the fellow I've heard so much about," Coach Ward said, shaking Townsend's hand vigorously. "It's a pleasure to meet you, young man.

Looks like Pine Ridge really knows how to develop quarterbacks."

"I hope so, sir," said Townsend.

"I do too, Jeff," replied Coach Ward. "Now, let's see. You've come a long way to see me—and the college, and it's getting pretty late. So what say to your coming with me? I've already alerted Mrs. Ward. Then, after supper, we'll have plenty of time to go through the college. There's a lot going on tonight, and I'm sure you won't be bored. Besides, we've got a lot to talk over."

"That sounds great, Coach, but Barbara here has to get back to Pine Ridge before it gets too late."

"Oh, I see."

Gene cleared his throat. "That's all right, Jeff," he said. "Barbara can ride home with us. We've got plenty of room."

Jeff looked at Barbara. "Is that all right with you, Barb?"

Barbara nodded, almost eagerly. "Of course, Jeff."

Townsend turned to the coach. "Okay, then. It's settled, and thanks for the invitation."

Townsend and the coach said their goodbyes then and hurried off. As soon as they were gone, Mr. Wittington announced the name of the restaurant where they were going; and when Gene's father started to protest a second time, Mr. Wittington silenced him quite simply. This was *his* treat, he told them.

The dinner was a fine one, and there was a warmth about the table that kindled the spirit just as the food satisfied their hunger. And when it was over, Fred and Gene's father had finally shaken hands on the deal to start a bakery in Pine Ridge, and Gene's mother was already beginning to dream about those fabulous new ovens.

They drove Skip back to his dormitory after the dinner, and everyone got out of the car to bid Skip goodbye; and Skip promised his parents at least a dozen times that he'd write more often. Then as they all started to get back into the car, Skip asked Gene to walk with him the rest of the way to the dormitory.

At first their conversation was strained and mechanical, and Gene knew that it was that letter hanging between them. Finally, when they reached the dorm steps, Skip stopped and looked down at Gene.

"I guess," he said, "we've got something to settle."

Gene nodded. "That letter I sent."

"That's right, Gene."

"I just wanted to be honest with you, Skip. I wanted you to know what a rat I was."

"Well, I'll tell you. At first I wasn't glad you sent it, Gene. I was pretty angry, I remember. I crumpled it up and threw it on the floor. I almost sat down and wrote *you* a letter. I was really steaming."

Gene nodded unhappily. It was not difficult at all to imagine how Skip must have felt.

"But then I thought it over," Skip went on, "and I figured how grateful I should be. You leveled with me, and now I knew what had been happening to me that weekend in Pine Ridge, why I couldn't seem to find you anywhere. Only a real friend would have had the guts to write a letter like that. You told it how it was. You didn't cover up. You didn't lie about it."

"Then we're still friends?"

"Sure we are. No matter what this crazy, hung-up world forces us to say or do."

"And that's a promise?"

"That's a promise, Gene."

Gene tried to reply, but he didn't trust his voice. Instead, he thrust out his hand.

Skip clasped it with both of his, shook it warmly, then turned and hurried up the stairs and into the dormitory. Gene watched the doors close behind him, stood there for a moment longer, then turned and walked back to the car.

Soon after they had left the lights of Hamilton behind, Gene became acutely aware of Barbara's nearness. They were sitting in the back seat alongside Fred Wittington, who was next to the window, his head resting back against the seat. Fred's eyes were open, and he was thinking, Gene was certain, of that wonderful game he had seen that day.

Gene smiled to himself at the thought.

"What are you smiling about?" Barbara asked softly.

Just as softly Gene replied, "I'm thinking of how proud Fred must be of Skip."

"Yes," she said. "It's wonderful he could have been there in the stands today. I suppose—I suppose it helps to make up for a lot."

Gene thought he knew what she meant by "a lot." He nodded. "I'm sure it does. I certainly hope so, anyway. And your being perfectly willing to ride back with me and my friends, the Wittingtons, also makes up for a lot, too. And it's about time."

"I know, Gene. It was mean and small of me. Jeff told me off when I told him about us. And he didn't mince any words either. I've been a silly goose. Please forgive me."

"Let's just forget it, Barbara. It's over now."

She rested her head on his shoulder then. "Wasn't this nice of Jeff?" she whispered.

"What do you mean?"

"Well, he was the one who suggested I come to the game with him, even though he knew the coach planned to have him stay for dinner and give him a tour of the college afterward."

"You mean he knew about that?"

"Sure. And he also knew how much I wanted another chance to ride with you and the Wittingtons in your father's car."

"Let me get this straight. You mean Jeff . . . !"

She placed a forefinger on his lips. "Shh," she murmured. "Let's just enjoy the ride."

Gene leaned back and tried to still his furiously racing thoughts. *Townsend?* Now how could he figure a guy like that? He'd like to try, though; but now, since it was common knowledge that Marble would be back in the lineup for the last two games of the season, it looked as if Gene would never get the chance—either to understand Townsend or to make the team as a regular.

He became aware then of the gentle weight of Barbara's head on his shoulder. He took a deep breath. After all, he told himself, a guy couldn't have everything.

11

GENE OVERTOOK TOWNSEND as they left the locker room between halves.

"Townsend, you seen Barbara?"

"No, I haven't. Isn't she out there with the rest of the cheerleaders?"

"No, she isn't."

"Well, I don't know where she is then. Besides, she's your responsibility now, isn't she?"

"I guess so, and for that I'd like to thank you."

Townsend stopped. "Thank me? What for?"

"You know what for. Barbara told me what a big surprise having to stay for a supper and that tour around State was."

"Oh, that. Well, don't thank me. Thank Barbara. Ever since that little disagreement we had at the dance, she's been—well, not very happy about me. She thinks I'm a great big bully. Know what I mean?"

"Yes, I know just what you mean. So why don't you grow up some more and stop hiding the nice guy—stop getting your kicks by sticking pins into people?"

"You mean people with gimpy legs?"

"Yes, I do."

"Look. Did it ever occur to you that I wouldn't get any kicks that way if you didn't ask for it?"

"*Ask* for it?"

"That's right. Ask for it. You've been using that leg of yours as a crutch to hide behind for a pretty long while. I'd say it's about time you grew up yourself and came out from behind it."

With that he spun around and continued on to the bench. Gene followed slowly, a slight frown on his face. Townsend's words, surprisingly enough, made a kind of rude sense. Was it true? Had Gene all these years been using his leg as an excuse? Was that why he made such an easy target?

Slumping down on the bench, he glanced along its length and saw Coach Linardi talking to Townsend and Marble. He looked away.

Marble had played the entire first half, and his welcome back to the starting lineup had been punctuated by a rising roar of welcome from the stands when he trotted out onto the field. His presence, however, had not appeared to help the Pine Ridge offense any. The Hornets had yet to score, while the Red Creek Crimson had scored once and kicked a field goal.

Looking back up the bench, Gene was surprised to see Townsend and the coach walking toward him.

"Gene," the coach began as soon as he reached him, "Jeff wants me to put you in this half."

Gene glanced in astonishment at Townsend, then back at the coach. "Sure, but what about Marble?"

"His knee's still not right yet. And besides, he simply doesn't have your speed. No one on the team does, as a matter of fact."

"Well sure! If you—and Townsend—think I can do it."

"I do," said Townsend. "If you'll remember something Skip told me to tell you."

"Skip?"

Townsend nodded. "He said to tell you that there's just two people out on that field when you're going out for a pass—you and the quarterback."

"He told you that?"

"And he said for you to make believe you were out playing catch with old Skip again."

"Well, that won't be easy, Townsend. You're not the quarterback Skip Wittington is."

"You don't have to tell me that."

Coach Linardi shook his head. "Okay, you two. Stop scrapping. Save that fight for the playing field."

"Sure," Townsend said.

Then he and the coach turned and walked back up the bench. Gene picked his helmet off the bench and pulled it down over his ears. He was glad he was going to get a chance to play, but he thought it highly unlikely that he would ever be able to catch a pass thrown by Townsend as easily as he had been able to catch a pass of Skip's.

Townsend's first pass to Gene late in the third quarter seemed to prove this point with discouraging finality. It was a down and out. Gene got his fingers on it, but when he tried to pull the football close to tuck it away, he lost it.

As he trotted back to the huddle, he kept his eyes from meeting Townsend's. Perhaps he should have hung on to that one. It had not been a bad pass, and it had led him perfectly. Townsend made no crack, however, even though the incomplete pass made it third and seven.

Ketchel carried off tackle for six yards. It was a yard short of the first down, but at this stage in the game Linardi let Townsend go for the first down. Townsend pitched out to Huff on a sweep around the right side. Gene upended a linebacker to help out, and Wendell got them the yard they needed and three more to put the ball on the Crimson's forty-five.

"Button-hook," Townsend told Gene. "To the inside. And hang on to this one."

Gene nodded.

As the huddle broke, Terry Lowden slapped Gene on the back. "Don't worry, Crazylegs. You'll hang on to this one."

Gene nodded his thanks and realized at that moment that it was Terry Lowden who had first referred to him as "Crazylegs" after he had made that fateful catch. *The* catch, he thought to himself as he assumed his three-point stance.

On the snap Gene flew past the linebacker and headed directly at the defensive back. As soon as the fellow broke back upfield to stay with Gene, Gene slammed on the brakes, whirled around, and charged back. The ball was in the air. It was high. Gene leaped and smothered the ball against his chest. Even before he came down, he was hit, the tackler's helmet burrowing into the small of his back. With a whoosh of expelled air, Gene slammed to the ground, the football still firmly in his grasp.

"Nice pass," said Gene as he rejoined the huddle and glanced across it at Townsend.

"Nice catch."

Everyone in the huddle noticed that exchange, but quickly erased the surprise from their faces as Townsend went over the next play.

It was a quick flair to Terry Lowden. Gene cleared out the right side as he raced downfield, and Terry made better than fifteen yards.

And that put them on the twenty-yard line.

Ketchel took the ball on the next play. It was a fullback draw through the left side of the line. He made like a rampaging bull and wasn't stopped until he was on the five-yard line. Huff then went up the middle and carried to the one.

Townsend took it over on a sneak.

The kick was good, but that still left them three points behind with only six minutes left to play.

Linardi decided against an on-side kick and directed Townsend to boot a long one. Townsend got his foot into it, all right. The Crimson back caught the ball on his ten, faked right, then tried to make headway up the left side of the field. A swarm of tacklers buried him on the twenty.

Three plays later the Crimsons were forced to punt from their eighteen. The ball carried to the fifty-yard line where Terry Lowden swept under it and raced downfield to the thirty before he was knocked out of bounds.

By this time the roar from the stands was so loud that it was difficult for Gene to hear his teammates unless they shouted.

Townsend glanced swiftly around the huddle. "Huff, let's try that quick opener."

"All right by me," said Wendell.

But Wendell got only one yard.

"So we try that famous fullback draw," said Townsend, glancing over at Ketchel.

"Over me," said the right tackle. Over me!"

"Sure, Bing," said Townsend.

But the right tackle had underestimated his opposite number, and Ketchel met a stone wall. Now it was third and eleven with only two and a half minutes left.

"Okay," said Townsend. "Everyone in the stadium knows I'm going to pass, so I'm calling a screen, Terry carrying, right side."

A screen depends on faking, and part of that responsibility belonged to Gene. He looked uncommonly eager as he dropped to his three-point stance, and as he bolted past the linebacker and cut down the sideline, he turned and waved his arm frantically.

Gene saw Townsend loft the ball expertly over the heads of the charging linemen into Terry Lowden's waiting arms. Lowden promptly exploded downfield with a covey of blockers in front of him.

He almost made the first down. Townsend asked for the chain to be brought in, and that stopped the clock. The length of the football separated them from the first down, and they had less than two minutes to go.

Townsend didn't need to query the bench. He knew Linardi wanted him to go for it. Keeping the ball, he burrowed like a mole into the line and made it with only inches to spare.

First and ten on the twenty-yard line, and a minute left in the game.

Townsend, down on one knee in the center of the huddle, looked up at the players. "We need a quick opener up the middle to keep them honest. Ketchel, we'll go with that draw."

But the Crimsons were waiting for Ketchel and threw him back for a two-yard loss.

Townsend glanced around the huddle and took a deep breath.

"Give it to Crazylegs," said the still-perspiring Ketchel.

Townsend looked at Gene.

"It's just the two of us," Gene said. "Remember? You throw it, I'll catch it."

Townsend hesitated only a minute. "Okay. Down and out. You'll get it as soon as you cross into the end zone."

Gene nodded.

"It'll be a play pass," Townsend said, looking at Huff. "I'll fake to you coming around the right side."

Huff nodded.

"On set."

Gene allowed no thoughts of success or failure to intrude into his icy concentration. He kept his mind blank. He was simply having a nice game of catch with Jeff.

Townsend's cry of "Set!" released Gene like an arrow from a bow as he sprang across the line of scrimmage, shoulder-faked to the inside, then moved swiftly outside and down the line. The defensive back raced quickly over. At once Gene ducked inside of him and lit out for the left corner of the end zone.

Looking back, he saw Townsend just releasing the ball. The pass was longer than Gene had expected. He increased his speed as he raced across the goal line and at the last moment leaped high into the air.

Snaring the ball in his upcurved arms, he pulled it to him and glanced down. He was still inside the end zone, but dangerously close to the sideline. Relaxing completely, he came straight down, both feet striking the ground within fair territory.

And then a runaway bulldozer slammed into him from behind. He coiled himself about the football and, through the storm of cheers, crashed to the ground.

Not long after, as they were outracing jubilant fans to the locker rooms, Townsend pulled up beside Gene. "Hey there, Crazylegs, that was some catch. Welcome to the team."

"Thanks, Jeff. You and Skip were right. On a

pass play there's really only the passer and the pass-catcher—two guys working together."

Townsend slapped Gene on the back and pulled ahead.

As Gene watched him go, he heard Skip Wittington's familiar voice call out to him.

"Hey, Gene! Hold up!"

Gene stopped and turned to see Barbara and Skip Wittington hurrying toward him through the crowd.

"A friend who lives in the next town offered me a lift down," Skip explained as he reached Gene. "I thought I'd like to see a Pine Ridge game with a friend of mine playing end. Nice game, Gene."

"Thanks, Skip."

"He almost missed the game," said Barbara, smiling at Skip.

Skip grinned. "My buddy's car broke down before we reached Pine Ridge. I tried calling my father. But he wasn't home. Neither was your father, Gene. So I called Barbara's dad."

"So Dad picked Skip up," Barbara finished, "and drove us both over to the game. That's why I didn't get here in time to join the cheerleaders."

"Well, I missed you. I wondered what you were doing."

"She was screaming her head off for you from the moment you entered the game; that's what she was doing," said Skip. "Look, you go on in now and get dressed. We'll meet you outside in the parking lot. I've got some real good news for Jeff about that scholarship, so bring him along, too, that is, if you two are on speaking terms."

Gene grinned as he started off. "We're on speaking terms, all right—finally."

And they were, Gene realized, as he headed into the building. The past was over and gone. The Golden Boy who had felt impelled to taunt Gene because of his limp had grown up—and that kid who had tried to hide behind a limp was now Crazylegs Merrill.